book 4

tim bowler
winner of the carnegie medal

BLADE

RUNNING SCARED

OXFORD
UNIVERSITY PRESS

OXFORD
UNIVERSITY PRESS

Great Clarendon Street, Oxford OX2 6DP

Oxford University Press is a department of the University of Oxford.
It furthers the University's objective of excellence in research, scholarship,
and education by publishing worldwide in

Oxford   New York

Auckland   Cape Town   Dar es Salaam   Hong Kong   Karachi
Kuala Lumpur   Madrid   Melbourne   Mexico City   Nairobi
New Delhi   Shanghai   Taipei   Toronto

With offices in

Argentina   Austria   Brazil   Chile   Czech Republic   France   Greece
Guatemala   Hungary   Italy   Japan   Poland   Portugal   Singapore
South Korea   Switzerland   Thailand   Turkey   Ukraine   Vietnam

Oxford is a registered trade mark of Oxford University Press
in the UK and in certain other countries

British Library Cataloguing in Publication Data

Data available

ISBN: 978-0-19-275559-9

1 3 5 7 9 10 8 6 4 2

Typeset in Frutiger by TnQ Books and Journals Pvt. Ltd., Chennai, India

Printed in Great Britain by CPI Cox and Wyman, Reading, Berkshire

Paper used in the production of this book is a natural,
recyclable product made from wood grown in sustainable forests.
The manufacturing process conforms to the environmental
regulations of the country of origin.

Blade is frightened. He's been badly injured and has escaped from one set of enemies only to be captured by another. But who are these new people and what do they want? Is it to kill him? Or do they have other plans?

Thoughts of Jaz keep haunting him and he's plagued by guilt from the past. Mary has told him to give himself up. But it's too late for that now. He's surrounded by big, new dangers, his strength is failing, and he's running scared . . .

The fourth title in this ground-breaking series from Tim Bowler, the Carnegie Medal-winning author of *River Boy, Starseeker, Frozen Fire* and *Bloodchild*. Blade isn't alone any more—but the threat that is pursuing him is as deadly as ever . . .

tim bowler

BLADE

RUNNING
SCARED

Other Books by Tim Bowler

Blade: Playing Dead
Blade: Closing In
Blade: Breaking Free

Midget
Dragon's Rock
River Boy
Shadows
Storm Catchers
Starseeker
Apocalypse
Frozen Fire
Bloodchild

For Rachel,
with my love

The night, the motorbike, the twisting lane. The beam from the headlights stabbing the dark. It might as well be stabbing me. Cos I'm dead all over again. I know it. I'm hurtling through blackness, perched on the back seat.

And I'm dead all over again.

I don't even know the rider. I heard his voice, caught his eyes under the helmet. That's all. But I know enough. I jumped on like he told me to. Right thing to do cos it got us past the grinks. But it's only putting death off for a bit.

Cos this guy's a grink too.

Trust me. I got too many enemies. And no friends. So work it out for yourself. This gobbo's trouble. Big trouble too, dangerous. You don't risk your neck like he did for nothing. He gritted it big time to get me away. So what does he want?

Whatever it is, Bigeyes, it'll be messy.

I'm guessing a contract job. I told you before there's different types of grinks. There's the ones who want me for stuff I know. Once they've tortured that out of me, they'll stiff me. And there's the ones who want me for stuff I've done. I'm hoping they'll just stiff me quick and sweet.

But I don't suppose I'll be that lucky.

I'm guessing this gobbo's one of the second kind. Sent by some spike from the past who's got a grudge against me. There's enough of 'em. I turned over too many slugs to have a quiet life. Maybe I turned over one of his crew. So he sent this gobbo to get me.

And now it's payback.

Going to be bad, Bigeyes, whatever happens. And I'm weak as piss now. Wound in my head's slamming me, body's blasted after all the chasing, and my mind's stuffed after seeing Jaz and talking to Mary. What's left to fight another grink?

Not much. Maybe not anything.

But I still got some kind of a chance. That's why I jumped on the bike. This way there's just two of us. For the moment anyway. Won't be for long but right now it's him against me. Better odds than before. So I'm clinging on and hoping. He's got to stop some time.

And that's when I'll know what to do.

Fight or run.

Or both.

We're still moving fast. This is some machine, I'm telling you, and the gobbo's some rider. I'll give him that. I'm checking him best I can. Big guy, solid. More beef than your average dronk. Glance behind me.

Thought so. Headlights coming after us. Only they're not motorbikes. They're cars. And there'll be more coming the other way in a minute. The grinks back there'll have mobiled their mates. Second wave, case I got through the first.

Like I just did.

So this motorbike gobbo's in trouble too, whatever he wants from me. And he'll have to do something soon cos the motorway's just ahead, and there'll be a reception committee. Only wait a second . . .

He's switched off the lights and we're slowing down. We're still moving but there's darkness all around now. I don't like this. Can't see a thing hardly. Glance back.

Headlights getting bigger. They're racing after us but they're still some way off. Lights ahead of us too now, coming from the direction of the motorway. But we're still running through darkness.

Only now we're turning off the lane. We've slipped through an open gate—I can just make it out—and we're bumping down a track with a field to the left and a fence to the right. Peer at the rider.

He hasn't looked round once, hasn't checked to see what I'm doing or who's following. He's bent forward like he's been from the start, his helmet gleaming. But that's all the light that's coming from us now.

The bike's as dark as the night.

We're still bumping along the track, and now there's another gate in front, open too, and we're through that, and we're on another track, heading towards some trees. Maybe that's it, Bigeyes. Maybe that's where his mates'll be waiting.

Where it all ends.

A club, knife, bullet. Cute little grave. No one'll find me if they do it right. Look behind me again. Lights flashing down the lane, both directions. None of 'em coming our way.

But they will. They'll know we haven't got as far as the motorway. They'll regroup and come looking. They'll search every gate and every field. Yeah, Bigeyes, they want me that bad. But I got other problems now.

Check round. Still too risky to jump off the bike. We're going slower but not so slow I won't hurt myself if I try and bunk it. Got to wait a bit longer. Track's come to an end but he's driving on. We're in among the trees, bouncing along, lights still off.

Then suddenly he pulls up.

We're in a little clearing. Nobody else around, nobody I can see anyway. I scramble off the bike, scuttle back a few steps. Guy glances round, climbs off, clicks the bike onto its stand. Stares at me through the slit in his helmet. Then he moves.

I edge back further, but not too far. Got to watch this gobbo every second. If he's working on his own, that's better for me but it's still bad. He's big and strong and I won't get away by running. Even if I wasn't weak, I couldn't outpace him.

Got to wait, watch, see what he wants.

He's stopped by the back of the bike but he's still looking this way. I'm watching him cute. There's something about this guy. I've only just noticed. Something in his manner. I've seen him before somewhere.

But I can't work out where.

We're both still now, both staring hard. Behind him, where the lane cuts towards the motorway, I catch the flash of headlights. I can't see the cars. They're hidden below the rise of the land. But I can see the beams. And this gobbo must know they're there too. But he's not looking at them. He's keeping his eyes on me.

I call over.

'You're either brave or stupid.'

He doesn't answer, just goes on staring at me. I peer through the darkness at the slit in his helmet. Can't make out his eyes from here but I got a sense of 'em. Maybe if I could see 'em better, I could work out where I've met him. But that means trigging closer and I'm not that big a dimp.

I nod towards the lane.

'They're going to want you now. Not just me.'

Again he doesn't answer. Just reaches out, opens the panier at the back of the bike and pulls out another helmet. Then, without warning, he flings it over. I don't try and catch it. Just let it land close to my feet, then bend down and pick it up. He closes the panier, steps in front of the bike, faces me across the clearing.

'What do you want?' I say.

He nods to the helmet in my hands.

'Put it on. You need to look legal.'

And then I get it. The voice. It wasn't enough before, when he told me to get on the bike. It was gruff and hurried and there wasn't time to think. But now it's different. Just those few words, but I can hear the drawl. And I know who it is.

He doesn't need to do any more. But he does anyway. He pulls off his helmet and lets me see his face.

It's Dig.

Dead Trixi's brother. Twenty years old and tough as two men. The guy who sliced my head with his knife.

And there it is again. He's pulled it out. The blade looks even bigger than it did when he slashed me. Maybe it's still got my blood on it.

I reach in my pocket, feel for Scumbo's knife.

It's there, ready.

Only I can't pull it out. It's no good, Bigeyes. I got those feelings back, like I had with Paddy, and that other grink. Only it's worse now. I can't even pull the knife out. If Dig throws his, he's got a free plug.

And he does. He throws it.

I watch it skin the dark as it streaks towards me. Don't know why I haven't moved. Maybe I want it to slam me. But it doesn't. It dips at the last moment and stabs into the grass between my feet.

I look down at it, then up at Dig.

He didn't miss. He aimed it there. He could have slotted me easy. I'm near enough. But he didn't. Why not? I already know, Bigeyes. It's cos he's confident I can't hurt him back. Even with his own knife.

I lean down, pick it up, study it. One mean blade. No wonder I got hurt when he slit me. Heavy too, much heavier than Trixi's flick-knife, or the one in my pocket. Once upon a time I'd have liked this shit.

Squeeze my hand round it, look at Dig, size him up. Move my arm back.

He stiffens.

I hold still. I want to see him scared. He owes me that. But he doesn't flinch. Just watches me for a moment, checks me over, then settles his body, lounges, waits.

He's got bottle. I'll give him that. I hate the guy but he's crack-hard.

I take a step towards him. He stiffens again. Now he's not sure. Now I've got him. But still he won't move.

I want him to step back, step aside, something. But he doesn't. Just waits like before, watching me in the darkness. Then he speaks, same low drawl.

'You ain't going to do it.'

I take another step forward. Still he doesn't move. I wait, watching him. I'm so close now I could hit him blind. He gives me the drawl again.

'You ain't going to do it. And you know it.'

I got pictures flooding my head again, and they're all faces. Paddy's face, and the scumbo in the hospital, and those two grinks I saw on the old dunny's staircase. All mocking me the same way. Cos I can't do it any more.

Can't kill.

And now Dig's face. How come he knows? Is it the grinks? Did they tell him? Or is it just me, standing here, showing it in my face? We're close enough now. He can see my eyes dead clear. Just as I can see his. Dead clear.

They're watching me cute, but they're quiet eyes, relaxed eyes. Not scared at all. I drop the helmet to the ground, whip the knife right back over my shoulder. Still he doesn't flinch. Still the eyes go on watching me. Then he shakes his head.

'Ain't going to happen. Cos you ain't standing much longer.'

He's right, Bigeyes. I'm swaying on my feet and the world's spinning again. I got pain blacking me over, and fear, and exhaustion. And there's more pictures splitting my head—sweet Becky, her dead face peering up, and all the others, the faces I can't bear to see. The faces that never go away.

And Dig's among them, watching.

I feel myself drop the knife. The faces start whirling,

the blackness deepens.

I don't remember falling, just waking up, I don't know how much later. I'm staring into Dig's face. He's holding me and I hate it.

'Let go,' I mutter.

He doesn't. I scream at him.

'Let go! Let go!'

I got new pictures flashing, pictures from the past, pictures that freak my heart.

'Let go! Let go! Let go!'

He still goes on holding me. I spit into his face. He twists his head away, carries me over to the motor-bike, dumps me on the passenger seat, wipes the gob off with his sleeve. I glare at him but I'm losing it again. I'm upright, sort of, but my head's still spinning and I can feel the blacko creeping back.

Dig speaks.

'Blade.'

His voice has turned into mist.

'You got to hold on,' he says. 'Got to stay conscious, you understand? Cos we got to start riding again. And if you lose it, you'll fall off.'

I can't see him at all now. I feel something over my

head. The helmet, he's putting it on me. Now my hands. He's grabbed hold of 'em.

'Don't touch me,' I say.

He takes no notice, moves my hands behind me, closes the fingers round something cold.

'It's the bike rack,' he says. 'Hold onto it.'

I grip the rack.

'Now your feet,' he says.

'Don't touch 'em. I know where they go.'

Again he takes no notice. Just plants my feet, climbs on in front of me, speaks again.

'Don't let go, boy. Or you're dead.'

He pauses, like he's waiting for me to say something. But I can't speak, Bigeyes. I can't even think. I'm losing everything. I got a little bit left in me. Maybe enough to hang on, maybe not. I don't really care now.

I just want him to ride.

Somewhere, anywhere.

Doesn't matter where it is now. Or what he wants from me.

'Ride,' I mutter.

He starts the engine. It brays like a monster. I can't

believe the grinks on the lane won't have heard it. But he's not heading their way. Even in this state, I can tell that. He's kicked off the stand and we're bumping on through the trees, lights still off.

I don't know where he's going, Bigeyes.

And you know what? I don't give two bells.

My eyes are closing and it's like I'm gone. I'm not Blade. I'm not a fourteen-year-old kid clinging to the back of a motorbike. I'm not anyone. I'm just a thought moving through darkness.

I like that.

A thought moving through darkness.

The world's gone, life's gone. Blade's gone.

I just hope he never comes back.

But he does. Course he does, damn the bastard. He's like a curse. Even as I flake, I feel him hovering. Like you, Bigeyes—hovering. And there's others too. And I'm not talking about Dig.

Something's happened. There's more nebs round me. Bike's gone. Don't know where. I remember the trees but that's it. Don't remember the journey after that or getting off. Just know I'm somewhere else, it's dark in my head, and I can't move.

And I'm scared.

I can hear voices but no words. And something else, kind of a drone. Keep thinking I should know what it is. But my head's bombed and my thoughts are sprung. They got no shape, no sense.

Like me.

Then a word. Clear as sky. And someone's speaking it.

'Jaz.'

And now a picture. The little girl's face. She's looking at me with those fairy eyes. Not smiling or crying, not telling me it's all right. Just watching. I don't know if she's real or in my head. Voice comes again.

'Jaz.'

It's not Jaz talking. It's some girl, older. I'm getting more pictures now. I'm starting to remember. I'm guessing where I am and who I'm with. But I still can't see 'em. All I got is Jaz. But that's OK. Cos she's all I want.

I try and speak.

'Jaz, I'm sorry, baby.'

She doesn't answer. Don't know if she heard. The other voice comes back.

'Jaz, come on.'

Jaz disappears and all I got is darkness again, and the blur of voices, and the drone in the background. I know what it is now. I know what's happening. I'm in a van. And Blade's still here, locked inside me. He'll never go away, Bigeyes, no matter how much I want him to.

Think I'm losing it again, going blacko like before. I can feel it swimming over me. And I want it now. I want to forget again. For a while I wasn't me and it was plum. The black tide washes in, sweeps me away, rolls me up.

But not for long.

I'm soon back, dumped where I was, like a piece of driftwood. And that's how it feels now. I'm floating. I go with the current. I got no control over anything. And I know the nebs I'm with, even if I can't see 'em. Engine's getting louder, and now there's other sounds.

Sirens.

Must be porkers everywhere. All these murders in the city. Maybe the sirens'll help a bit, keep the grinks back. Getting louder, one of 'em. Louder, louder, louder. Dead close now, blaring over us, and light from the headlamps flooding the van.

Sound of voices nearby. I recognize 'em good this time.

The trolls talking.

'They're getting too close.'

'Might not be after us.'

'They is.'

'Might be turning off.'

'They ain't. They're checking us out.'

Another voice, a guy in the front.

'They're turning off.'

And the light fades away, taking the siren with it.

Something's touching my head, dabbing at me, something soft. Doesn't feel like a hand but I can't make it out.

'Stay still.'

Tammy's voice. No missing that. She's taken over as leader, now Trixi's dead. Don't ask me how I know. Sash won't like it. Nor will Xen and Kat. But they won't challenge her. She was always the strongest after Trixi.

Not that any of that's going to help me. Trolls are

trolls and this crew's always hated me. If they're patching me up, it's only so I'm fit for something worse.

'Stay still,' says Tammy.

I didn't know I was moving.

'Open your eyes,' she says.

Didn't know they were closed either. I open 'em. Still blackness all around me. No faces, just shapes. Then one, clear. Not Tammy or any of the other trolls. It's Jaz again. And she's real. She's right next to me.

'Jaz,' I whisper.

I can feel my mind splitting again and the blacko coming back. Got to keep it away. Got to keep my eyes on Jaz. She reaches out, pats at my forehead, and then I know what's been dabbing me. She's holding an old sweater. Tammy's voice again.

'Your wound's bleeding.'

And now her troll-face, glaring down. I always hated it. Spitty eyes, no friends of mine. She looks me over, growls.

'Keep still.'

Glances at Jaz.

'Give me the thing.'

Jaz hands her the sweater. Tammy nods towards the front of the van.

'Go back and sit with Riff.'

Jaz disappears. I close my eyes, feel the sweater on my brow again.

'You should be dead,' says Tammy.

'Why aren't I?'

'Good question.'

Yeah, Bigeyes, good question. She's right. I should be dead. Breaking free should have cost me my life. But maybe it has. Maybe the next blacko'll be it. The one I don't come back from.

I thought I was dead before. In the ambulance, in the hospital, in Scumbo's black arms. And then later— on the rooftops, in the streets, running, running. But how long can you run when you're hurt that bad?

Cos I was, and I still am. I know that.

'Bleeding's gross,' says Tammy.

I don't answer. She's not talking to me anyway.

'Tam?' says Sash.

'What?'

'Can't you stop it?'

'I'm trying, aren't I?'

'I was just asking.'

'You wasn't. You was telling me I'm doing a shit job.'

'Hey!' calls Riff from the front of the van. 'Shut it, you two!'

'You shut it,' says Tammy.

'You babes are always rowing.'

'So what?'

'So don't,' says Riff. 'You know Dig hates it.'

'Well, he ain't here, is he?' says Tammy. 'So piss off!'

Riff says no more. Sash speaks, low voice.

'Bleeding's getting worse.'

No answer from Tammy, just the feel of the sweater again, and the blood flowing down my face. The sirens seem far away now. I can still hear 'em but they're like voices from another world. Here comes the blacko again.

At last.

Come on, mate. Fold me up. I've had enough of this. And I don't mean the trolls slugging, or the pain, or the stuff they got waiting for me. I mean everything. Every thing. Let the blood flow all it wants.

Cos you know what, Bigeyes? I owe it. Too right I

do. I owe more blood than I got in my body. Maybe if it all drains away, I'll have given something back. Not enough for what I owe. Not by a long way. But maybe enough to get a bit of peace.

And there's something else too.

I'll be dead.

And you don't get more peaceful than that.

Light. Consciousness. A new movement. A new kind of fear.

I'm on water.

I can tell. I'm alive and I'm on water. Wound's stopped bleeding but something else is running down my cheek. It's sweat. Got my eyes wide open but all I can see is a blur. Light's clear but nothing else is. Just the feeling of water.

And my fear of it.

'Drowning.'

I'm murmuring. I can hear my own voice. Doesn't sound like me. Sounds like some dungpot with his head banged in. But it is me. I know it. More sweat. I can feel the beads on my neck now.

Close my eyes, open 'em again.

Light's still there, but now I can see stuff. Inside of a cabin: small, smoky, little round portholes. I'm lying on a bunk with a blanket over me. I don't remember coming here. Nobody else with me. Nobody I can see anyway.

But I'm not alone.

There's sounds coming from behind my head. Twist round. Painful to move but I manage it. Closed door that way, another cabin probably. And the sounds are coming from there. No mistaking what's going on.

Some couple making out.

Twist my head back. Boat rocks. Feel my body tense. Another rock of the boat. I start to tremble. I can feel the water close, like it's breathing up through the boat—into my face, into my heart.

'No!' I scream.

Sounds break off in the other cabin. Door opens, figure stumbles out. Riff, doing up his trousers. Another figure, one of the trolls. Can't remember her name. I'm still drowning in my head. She straightens her kit, puts a hand on my cheek.

'Lay off!' I snarl.

She takes her hand away. I glare at her. Name comes back. Kat, that's it. She's watching me close. Gritty eyes but better than Tammy's. Snap of warmth in 'em. Not much but a bit. And she can do better than Riff for a bed-bum.

Check him out, Bigeyes. Proper slimeball. I'm not forgetting he shunted me with Paddy and those other grinks. Question is—what's his jig now? I got to think, got to hold back this fear. I'm out of strength. Got no spit left in my body.

But I'm still alive. Don't ask me why. And there's another thing.

Where's the rest of the gang?

Riff answers my question like I spoke it out loud.

'There's nobody else here. Just me and Kat.'

I don't answer. I'm still trying to think.

'You screamed,' says Kat. 'What's up?'

Still don't answer, still trying to think. Sound of an engine roaring past. Riff checks through the porthole, looks back.

'Nothing,' he says to Kat.

Then the swell hits us. Boat starts to rock. I can't help it. I'm screaming again.

'No! No!'

'Easy,' says Kat.

She reaches out.

'Don't touch me!'

'OK, OK.' She takes her hand away, stands back.

Both watching me now, narrowed eyes, like they don't know what to do. Sweat's pouring down me like a flood. Boat settles and I calm down a bit.

'Blade,' says Riff.

'Shove it.'

'Blade, listen.'

I scowl at him. He takes no notice, leans forward. I see his eyes clear. Dark little dots, flicking about. He smiles. But it's not a proper smile. Just a mouth moving. Like the eyes. Fixed on nothing, worth nothing.

'You're ill, Blade.'

'Shove it.'

'You're ill. You're badly hurt. I know why you're scared. You think we're going to kill you. Well, we ain't. We know about Trixi. We know who killed her. We know it wasn't you.'

I turn my head away. I can't bear to look at these two. I just want 'em to go. I want to think, make sense of all this, deal with the water, deal with what's in my head. I hear Kat speak, but not to me. She's whispering to Slimey.

'He's scared stiff.'

Riff grunts.

'Blade?' says Kat. 'We ain't going to hurt you.'

I'm trembling again. Can't stop. If I could just get off this water. But I'm stuck here, too weak to move, too weak to think almost. It's not just the wound Dig fizzed in my head. It's what it cost me breaking free.

Cos it was everything, Bigeyes. Everything I had. And all for this, all for nothing. There's just one thing left worth caring about now. I turn my head back to 'em.

'Where's Jaz?'

Kat and Riff look at each other.

'Where's Jaz?' I say.

Kat answers.

'Bex is looking after her.'

I close my eyes. It's good for a moment cos I can see the little girl's face in the darkness. Not smiling but safe. Safe in my head anyway. Then I feel something on my cheek. It's not Kat's hand. It's something cold.

Familiar.

'Take it away,' I say.

I don't open my eyes. I just wait. It stays there for a moment, then goes away. I open my eyes and see Riff closing the blade of the flick-knife. The one I had in my coat pocket. Along with the other stuff.

'I was trying to show you,' he says.

'Show me what?'

'That we're not going to hurt you. I was trying to give you back your knife.'

'I had my eyes closed. How would I know you weren't trying to slit me?'

'But I didn't, did I? Like you say, you had your eyes closed. You were an easy target. If I'd wanted to cut your throat, we wouldn't be talking now.'

His eyes dance over me.

'Here,' he says. He holds out the knife, closed now. 'I just wanted to make you see what I'm doing. So I can give this back to you.'

I don't take it. He rests it on the bunk, straightens up.

'So you've been through my pockets?' I say.

He doesn't answer, just glances at Kat. I try again.

'What you done with the other stuff?'

'Like what?'

'Like the other stuff.'

'You mean the twelve and a half grand?'

'Yeah. I mean the twelve and a half grand.'

He shrugs.

'Call it rent.'

'You bastard.'

'For safe custody.'

'You bastard.'

The eyes stop moving for a second, then flicker on.

'You might think it money well spent,' he says, 'when you consider how much danger we're keeping you from.' He leans closer. 'There's police everywhere looking for you. And God knows how many other people. Nasty people too. We don't know who they are. Maybe you're going to tell us.'

'Maybe I'm not.'

'Whoever they are, they're not very friendly. But you don't need me to tell you that, do you?'

The boat rocks again. I clutch the side of the bunk and my hand touches the knife. I close it inside my grip, squeeze it tight. Boat goes on rocking, then slowly settles again. I hold up the knife, flick it open.

Kat stiffens. Riff just smiles.

'There's no point hurting us, Blade. Cos we're all that's keeping you safe now. You need us on your side.' He shakes his head. 'Look at you. You're wounded. You're knackered. And you're running scared.'

I stare at the blade for a moment, then twist my hand and slam the point down into the bunk. The knife quivers for a few seconds, then falls still. I glower up at Riff.

'You'll be running scared soon. And the rest of your crew.'

'And why's that?' he says.

I pause, fix 'em both.

'Cos the shit that's coming after me's coming after you now.'

They feed me: sandwiches from a polybag, couple of apples, unripe banana. Give me a bottle of mineral water. I eat, drink a bit, fall asleep. When I wake, it's dark again, and I'm alone.

Except for you, Bigeyes. And the stinky water. I got a woolly hat on my head and the bandage is still on.

Or maybe it's another bandage. Don't know. It's wet anyway.

I'm on my feet—managed that after a struggle—but I got nothing in my legs. Nothing much anyway. Just enough to stand, check out the boat, slop over to the porthole, stare out.

Familiar sight. Moorings, boats swinging with the tide, lights from the shore quarter of a mile away. I know this place well enough. Back end of the city, where the river gobs into the sea. But I've never seen it from the water before.

Don't have to tell you why.

Least I've stopped trembling. That's one good thing. But I still choke up every time the boat heaves. And it does that a lot. This is one slaggy tub. Supposed to be a motor cruiser but it's more of a floating wreck. Two dronky cabins and a wheelhouse. Smell of diesel and rotting timber. Bits of rope and chain. Stuff all else.

And no dinghy to get me ashore.

I don't remember Riff and Kat going. Must have been sleeping when they split. But I'm glad they've gone. I might be stuck here on my own but it's about as safe as anywhere else right now, long as I stay inside the cabin.

And I'm cute about that. You better believe it. Cos I'm telling you, Bigeyes, there's no way I'm going out on deck, not with the water that close. I can just about handle it from in here. So I'll slap it in the cabin for now. I got to stay out of sight anyway.

Just wish I could stay out of mind too. Cos that's the crack of it, Bigeyes. I'm in too many people's heads now. Porkers, grinks, you name it, all sniffing my tracks. I got to watch every shadow.

Something's moving on the water.

Can't see it yet but I can hear an engine. Not loud, just an outboard motor probably, some way off. Coming from the right. Check out the portholes. Nothing. Just the water and the lights from the shore.

Boat's getting closer. Still quiet, just a hum, but it's slowing down. There it is. Black shape moving through the moorings. I was wrong. It's not got an outboard motor. It's a launch with a little doghouse and a chuggy engine down below.

Three figures in the cockpit.

One of 'em's the grunt.

There's no missing that gobbo. Even in the dark I can see his fat face. Check round, reach for the bunk. Knife's still stuck in it. Pull it out, squeeze the handle, turn back to the porthole.

Launch has slowed down further but it's still moving. Not coming this way but weaving about, checking the moored boats inshore. I'm watching cute. They're over by the cruiser with the tatty awning.

Peering through the portholes.

One of 'em's climbing on board, checking under the cover. Now he's back in the launch. Rev of the engine and they're off again, but only to the next boat. And it's same again.

Shit, Bigeyes. If they check this dingo, I'm clemmed.

And they will. They're grubbing out all the bigger boats. They'll do this one too. Least I got no lights on. And the grinks don't seem to know which boat I'm on cos they're slugging all of 'em. Some screamer's tipped 'em off, I reckon, but not with any details or they wouldn't be checking rough-cut.

Even so, I got to hide.

Only where? Cabins won't do, nor will the wheelhouse. Loo's too obvious. So there's one choice left and it's a bum gripe. I'm not going there till I know I got to. Peer out the porthole.

Careful.

Got to keep 'em in view but stay out of sight. Yeah, they're checking everything. Not just the big boats now. They're even grubbing out the little 'uns. Just a poke in but enough to make sure.

They're coming this way.

Quick!

Knife down, coat on, knife back in my hand, check round. Just the food and mineral water to show 'em I was here. Shove the banana skin and apple core into the polybag. Stuff it in one pocket, bottle in the other.

Engine's getting louder.

Creep to the front of the cabin, up into the wheelhouse, keeping low. Pause, listen. They're almost alongside now. Down into the engine room. Only it's not an engine room. It's a greasy cupboard you wouldn't force a rat in.

But I got to hide there.

Somehow.

Ease my body in, twist it round over the engine,

close the little door after me, hold it tight. As I do so, I hear the grinks climb on board.

All three. I'm sure of it. Starboard side's gone right down. Even the grunt couldn't do that on his own. Engine's still chugging alongside but I'm guessing they've tied up and come aboard.

Three grinks.

And me.

Shit.

Footsteps on the deck. Boat's back on an even keel. The grinks are spreading about. In a moment they'll see the hatchway's open and find their way down into the cabins. Then they'll check out the wheelhouse.

And the engine room.

A voice, clear over the sound of the engine. And I know it at once. That familiar grunty sound.

'Hatchway's unlocked.'

Sound of the hatchway being pulled back. Footsteps thumping down into the cabin I was in. Bang of a door as someone checks the other cabin. Another bang as he comes out again. More footsteps.

Heading for the wheelhouse.

There's three of 'em. I was right. I can tell from the footsteps. First grink's in the wheelhouse, now the second, now the third. I can see one of 'em through a gap in the door. Just a tiny bit, the outside of a boot.

In a moment the door's going to yank open.

And they'll have me.

Grunt speaks.

'I can see him.'

'Blade?' says another.

'Yeah.'

'Where is he?'

He's playing with me, Bigeyes. And he's playing with his mates. He's spotted the little door. They all have. You can't miss it. But he's the one who's worked out I'm behind it. He must have seen me through the gap. Squeeze my hand round the knife.

If I can just get some of my old bottle back . . .

It's a long shot and they'll still get me. But I might be able to take one of 'em first. Grunt speaks again.

'There.'

He's got to be pointing down at the door.

'On the shore,' he says. 'See?'

No answer from his mates, just a rush of footsteps,

a smash of the wheelhouse door as they blast it open, then a rev of the engine.

And they're powering off towards the shore.

Jesus, Bigeyes, I'm thanking that guy. The guy they think is me. I just hope nothing happens to him. But whoever he is, I owe him.

OK, got to hold on a bit, got to wait.

Got to be sure. Engine's fading quick cos they're ripping up. That's good cos I want 'em gone, but I still got to wait. Got to play stealth. No matter how much I hate this cupboard.

Give it another minute. Got to be sure, dead sure. Another minute, another. Now it's cute. Shove open the door, fall back into the wheelhouse. I'm rolling on the floor, breathing hard, and—shit, Bigeyes. I'm crying again.

What's the matter with me?

I can't crack this, Bigeyes. The tears and stuff. I never used to cry. Not after I toughed out. Up to age seven, yeah. Tears, plenty of 'em. Then nothing. Not a drop, not even when Becky died. I wanted to but I knocked 'em back. You got to do that or you're bombed.

Are you listening to this, Bigeyes?

You knock 'em back or they knock you back. You're finished. You don't make it. Only now I can't stop 'em. Ever since the grinks came back, and Bex and Jaz and Mary came into my life, it's like they brought the tears with 'em.

So now what?

Stay alive. That's what. Cos I'll tell you something, Bigeyes. It's not about winning. It's about staying alive. You know why? Cos you don't win against these nebs. Most of the time you don't stay alive either.

Not if you go against 'em. There's too many grinks out there. And too many spikes pulling their strings. And up above the spikes, the meanest slime of the lot. We're talking serious shit, Bigeyes. Trust me. Serious shit. And it's not just this country.

It's global.

I'm telling you, there's nebs out there with everything to lose if I stay free. Why? Cos there's stuff I know, stuff they want, stuff other people want, including the porkers. But that's not the most dangerous thing. The most dangerous thing is something I don't know.

The person at the very top.

But never mind that now. I got to crash these tears, get my head straight, check Grunty and his mates have gone. Over to the wheelhouse door. It's hanging limp, half-off its hinges. Keep low, peer out.

There's the launch, moored up against the old barge. No sign of the grinks. They didn't hang about. Must have climbed ashore and run after the guy they thought was me. So I got to be careful and keep watching.

Cos when they find out it's not me, they'll come back.

And go on looking.

They might even come back here.

I hate this, Bigeyes. I feel so trapped. And I hate this water. It feels closer than ever now with the door pushed out of the way. I can see its black face right in front of me. Maybe it can see mine. Maybe I'm not the only one who's scared. Maybe the water's scared too. Scared of me even.

Don't think so though.

'Are you scared of me?' My voice sounds weird. Like a whisper and a scream at the same time. 'Eh? Are you scared?'

The water doesn't answer. Just wrinkles its dark skin. I shiver.

'I'm scared of you. I don't mind admitting it. I'm cute about that.'

A ripple runs over the surface, dies under the boat.

I push the door back further, bend down closer to the deck, edge myself over the threshold. I'm on hands and knees now. Can't bring myself to stand. Not just cos the grinks might see me if they come back. If they weren't around, I'd still be on hands and knees.

And you know why.

Inch towards the gunwale, still close to the deck. Don't ask me why I'm doing this. Maybe if the water told me it was scared too, I'd be braver. But it hasn't so I'm not. But I got to get closer somehow.

Got to stare this bastard down.

Ease myself further. I'm flat out now, pulling myself over the deck, eyes tight shut. I didn't want 'em like that, but I can't help it. They closed by themselves and I can't force 'em back open.

Never mind.

I'll do it in a minute. When I get there. Just a bit further. I'm moving slower, fighting the will to stop, but then suddenly I'm there. I can feel my head brushing the gunwale. The timber's chafing against my wound.

A jet of pain runs through me.

And I open my eyes.

And there below me is the water, just a hand's reach away. But my hands are nowhere near it. I got a ring-bolt in one and a bollard thing in the other, and I'm clasping 'em tight. But my head's over the side of the boat and I'm looking down into that black face.

'You laughing at me, dungpot?'

The water gurgles against the side of the boat.

'You are laughing.' I spit down into it. 'Laughing at my fear.'

Sound of an engine jerks my eyes back up.

The launch is moving again. Christ, Bigeyes, what am I doing? I should've been watching for this. And now I'm stuck out here. Least I'm lying down. But if they come this way, I'm plugged.

They don't.

Thank God. They're heading off down the river.

Watch 'em go, chug, chug, chug. Yeah, go on, grinks. Wig it all the way to hell. They hit the bend, disappear round it, and they're gone.

I look back at the water below me.

Same squinty face.

'You're still laughing at me.' I spit into it again. 'Well, I don't care. Here, have some food.'

I pull the polybag out of my pocket, reach down and let the water fill it. The apple cores and banana skin swim round inside like dronky fish. I let go the bag and it slips from view. I snarl at the water.

'Thirsty, are you?'

I pull out the bottle of mineral water.

'Want some of this, claphead?'

It's almost full. I only had a couple of sips before I fell asleep. I let it drop. It gives a little splash and then slips away too. And now it's just me again. Me and the black face laughing up. Like it doesn't give two bells if I live or die.

I pull out the knife, flick it open, stare down at the water again.

'If I could kill you, I would.'

Another ripple on the surface. Another gurgle

against the side of the hull. I let the knife fall. It stabs the black face and goes straight down. I feel the tears start again, pull myself back from the edge, stand up.

And see a new boat moving on the river.

Crouch down again, peer out. A rowing boat, small, more of a dinghy. One person in it. Can't see who. Too dark. No splashing with the oars, just an even stroke. Whoever it is knows how to row. Ease back into the wheelhouse, still low, still peering out.

Dinghy's coming this way.

No question about it. No weaving about to check the other boats. This neb's heading for me. Least it's just one person. One against one if it bloods up. But now I can see who it is.

Bex.

Don't know if I'm pleased or angry. I want to get off this tub. But I don't want to spend time with that troll. Not after she lied about Jaz. She zipped me over too bad with that. And I won't forgive her.

But I suppose I can crack a few minutes with her if it gets me ashore.

Trouble is, I got a feeling it's going to be more than a few minutes. Cos the truth is, Bigeyes, I still haven't got any strength. Not enough to wig it anyway. And there's no way Bex is on her own. She's rowing out by herself but there's got to be others waiting on shore.

And I won't get away from them.

But never mind that now. First things first. Get off this tub. Get back to the shore. Then decide what to do. She's getting closer. Handling that dinghy like a pro. I'll give her that. Guess there's one thing she can do well, apart from lie.

She's just a short way off now. Stops rowing, spins the boat round so she's facing me, shouts over the water.

'Blade!'

Yeah, troll. Tell the whole world I'm here.

'Come out the wheelhouse,' she calls, 'and go down the stern. It's easier to get in the dinghy from there.'

I can't believe this dreg. She's just rowed straight out here and now she's popping her mouth for everyone to hear. She's not even looking round to check for trouble. I got to stop this before she does something worse.

I bustle out on deck, growl down at her.

'Don't make so much noise.'

'There's nobody 'ere.' She looks up at me like I'm a tick. 'River's empty. Get down the stern.' She nods towards it. 'The back.'

'I know where the stern is,' I mutter.

She doesn't answer. She's already pulling towards it. We get there same time.

'Jump in,' she says.

I stare down. Dinghy's bobbing like a ball. I'm not getting in that.

'What's wrong?' she says.

'Nothing.'

'You're trembling.'

I don't answer.

'It's no big deal,' she says. 'Water's calm.'

It's not, Bigeyes. It was calm before but now it's bucking like hell. Don't shake your head. It's bucking like hell, OK?

'Just climb on the edge,' she says, 'and stick your bum on it. Then ease your feet down into the dinghy. I'll help you.'

'No, you won't.'

I climb onto the edge, sit down.

'I'll guide your feet,' she says.

'Don't touch me.'

I ease myself down, still clinging to the side of the motorboat. Bex grabs my feet before I can kick her hands away and steers them to the bottom of the dinghy.

'Let go the motorboat and sit down,' she says.

I slump onto the thwart in the stern of the dinghy.

'Jesus,' she mumbles. 'What a fuss.'

'Just row.'

She starts to row back towards the shore. I don't speak. I can't. I got nothing I want to say to Bex anyway but that's not it. I'm choked up to my brains with the water so close.

'You OK?' she says.

'Why shouldn't I be?'

'You're gripping the thwart like your life depends on it.'

'Just row, OK? And shut your mouth.'

She does one but not the other.

'Don't know why you're slagging me off. I ain't done you no harm.'

'You lied about Jaz.'

'And you never lied to me?' She stops rowing, fixes me. 'You done nothing but lie.'

'How do you know?'

'I just do.' She glowers at me. 'You saying I'm wrong?'

I shrug.

'You ain't told me nothing,' she says. 'Nothing much anyway. Nothing about them guys what's after you. Nothing about who you is or what you done. And how much of what you have told me's true, eh? Shit all, I'm guessing.'

I look away.

'Shit all,' she says.

And she goes on rowing.

Yeah, I know, Bigeyes. She's right. But I still hate her. And I'm too tired to argue about it any more. I just want to lie down, somewhere safe. But I reckon that's too much to hope for tonight. Still, as long as Bex keeps quiet for a bit.

But that's too much to hope for too.

'I come to get you cos of them guys in the launch.'

I look back at her.

'We seen 'em,' she says. 'Me and Dig. We was on the shore. Coming to bring some more food. And check you out.'

She's watching me close. Can't read her face. She's not angry any more. I can tell that much. But I can't tell the rest. I think she wants me to trust her. Like I'm ever going to do that.

She's still watching me.

'Dig sent me to bring you in,' she says. 'He reckons them guys might come back cos they didn't finish checking all the boats. So we got to take you somewhere else tonight.' She glances over her shoulder, then back at me. 'Only we don't know where. Just know you can't stay on the boat.'

'Whose is it?'

'Jojo's dad's. This dinghy's his too.'

'Who's Jojo?'

'Xen's boyfriend.'

'So that's two more people you told about me.'

Bex shakes her head.

'Jojo just knows we're helping some kid. His dad don't know nothing.'

I don't like it, Bigeyes. I don't like it one bit. But

there's nothing I can do. And I'm feeling dizzy again, like the blacko's coming back.

'Blade?' says Bex.

'What?'

'You don't look too good.'

'Thanks.'

'Your forehead—'

'What about it?'

'Just looks . . . '

I reach up, feel the bandage. It's still on, underneath the woolly hat. But they're both wet.

'I know,' I say. 'Looks gross.'

'Dig feels bad about it.'

'Bit late for that now.'

She doesn't answer. We're close to the shore and she's checking over her shoulder. I can see a figure over by the landing stage to the left. But it's not Dig. It's one of the trolls.

Xen.

Check round for the others. No sign of anyone. But I can see the van parked up the road. Same one Riff was driving. Bex is pulling towards the landing stage. I look at her.

'How come it's just you fetching me?'

'Cos the others ain't much good at rowing.' She sniffs, wipes her nose on her sleeve, rows on. 'And I am.'

'How come?'

'I was born by the sea. And my bastard dad used to get me to row him out to his sailing cruiser.' She sniffs again. 'Only he never wanted to do no sailing.'

She goes quiet, looks away, looks back. And suddenly I read her face clear, like I can see everything she wants to say, but can't. I stare at her, swallow hard. I want to tell her I'm sorry. I want to tell her I get it. But she speaks first, in a quick, hard voice, like she wants to stop me.

'There's another reason it's just me.'

'Yeah?'

'Dig says it don't look so suspicious.'

I still want to speak. Say sorry. Cos I know where she's been, Bigeyes. Sort of. Wasn't the same for me. Different circumstances. But the same result. I look at her, open my mouth—but she glares at me and I know she doesn't want to hear.

Check round again. No other figures, no movement.

Just Xen waiting on the landing stage, hands in her pockets.

'What time is it?' I say.

Bex isn't listening. She's checking over her shoulder again as she pulls in.

'Bex, what time is it?'

'Christ knows,' she mutters. 'Ten, eleven, whatever.'

I look round again. Water, boats, shore. No sign of anyone, apart from Xen and us. But I'm telling you, Bigeyes, I can feel nebs everywhere. Grinks, porkers, God knows who else. And they're close. Don't ask me how I know.

Bex brings us alongside the landing stage, glances at me.

'You can stop clutching the thwart now.'

Xen looks down, sparky face, sparky eyes, bit like Kat's only harder. Don't go for this troll. Don't trust her. And I'll tell you something, Bigeyes. I might be ill, might be weak, might be missing stuff, but there's one thing I can see.

She's no friend of Bex's. I can tell. And it's mutual.

Look at 'em both. Gut flush, eyes ripping. But never mind that. Here's Dig leaning down. Didn't see him get out the van, hit the landing stage. That scares me.

I don't mean seeing him. I mean not seeing him. I never used to miss stuff like that. But I didn't see him move, and here he is. And now I'm slotting something else, something about the two trolls. The way they're looking at him.

OK, I get it. Probably Dig does too. Probably he likes it. But who gives two bells? Not me, Bigeyes. It's their problem. I'm too blasted to bother. All I want is to get off this etting water and crash somewhere. Never mind a snug. Just leave me in the van. I'm past caring.

'Get him out the dinghy,' says Dig.

Don't know how they sting it. I certainly don't help 'em. But somehow I'm up on the landing stage, and I'm standing, kind of, and Dig's half-pulling, half-carrying me to the van. And you know what?

I don't even mind that. Him touching me and all. I'm so wiped I hardly notice. I hear the back door of the van open, feel myself pushed in, hear the door close, and now it's dark. Someone's next to me. Don't know who.

Wish it was Jaz.

But it's Bex. I can see now. Twist my head round, peer towards the front. Dig's in the driver's seat, Xen next to him. And there's that look again. Hers on him. I don't clock Jojo's chances with her. But I'll tell you something else.

I don't clock hers on Dig either.

Cos one thing's bung-clear: Dig's got someone else now. Someone he had before. Someone who's now forgiven. There's no missing it. I lie down, murmur to Bex.

'You're back with Dig.'

She doesn't answer. I close my eyes.

'Bex?'

'What?'

'You spoken to the police?'

'No.'

'They're looking for you.'

'They're looking for all of us,' she says. 'You, me, and Jaz.'

'But you and Jaz aren't missing any more. You're

back. So what did you tell the police? They must have been round asking questions.'

'Ain't told 'em nothing. Kept out of the way when they come. Kept Jaz out of the way too.'

'So they think you're still missing?'

'Yeah.'

'And Jaz?'

'Yeah.'

I don't like this, Bigeyes. What Bex does is her business. I know she's scared of the porkers cos she told me that once before. But Jaz is another matter. I hate the little kid getting mixed up in all this. But I can't think of any of that now.

Dig calls back.

'Pull the blanket over him.'

Bex does what he says. It smells mouldy but it's warm. Dig calls out again.

'Keep him out of sight. Keep him lying down.'

I got no problem with that, Bigeyes. Cos I'm not moving. Dig starts the engine and we pull away. I feel Bex lean closer. But I keep my eyes shut.

'You got to stay down,' she says.

I don't answer. She goes on.

'There's police everywhere. And other weirdoes. Like them guys. You probably know who they are. But I suppose you ain't telling us.'

I say nothing. I can feel the darkness wrapping me up. And it's plum.

'Shit!' says Dig suddenly.

'What?' says Bex.

'Police cars. And a motorbike.'

I keep my eyes closed, pull the woolly hat down over 'em. Don't know why I'm not whammed about the crap outside. Maybe it's cos I know there's nothing I can do. I got no strength to fight or run. I'm stuck here and I'm cute about it for the moment. No decisions to make. It's Dig's gripe. He's spinning the wheel now and whisking us off down another street.

But he's soon muttering again.

'Bloody hell. More of the bastards.'

He spins the wheel again and we drive on, cutting left, cutting right, cutting everywhere, and so it goes on, road after road, change after change, till I hear the groan of the brakes again. And the sound of Dig pounding the wheel.

'Christ, they're stopping the traffic now. I can see 'em up the road.'

'How many's out there?' says Bex.

Xen gives a snort.

'You blind or something?'

Bex snaps back an answer.

'Course I ain't! But I weren't looking that way.'

'Then turn your 'ead.'

'I'm keeping an eye on Blade.'

'What for? He's asleep, ain't he?'

'Dunno.'

'Well, he ain't moved or done nothing for ages.'

'Hey!' Dig snarls at 'em. 'Stop the bickering. I got to think. Got to work out how to get round the police cars.'

'Sorry, Digs,' says Xen.

There's a silence. Goes on and on. Like none of 'em wants to break it. Cos none of 'em knows what to do. I call out.

'Cut left into Adams Street. Take the little lane halfway down on the right. There's just enough room to get the van through. Then cut back down St Stephen's Gardens and you'll be round the police.'

More silence. Just the sound of the engine ticking over. Dig speaks.

'How come you know where we are?'

I don't answer.

'Eh?' he says. 'You been lying there with that hat over your eyes since we left the river. I seen you in the mirror. You ain't moved once. And we changed roads like I don't know how many times.'

Yeah, Diggy, wonder all you want. But if you knew the city like I do, you'd know it's a spit to keep a check on the roads you just took. All of 'em. Even with my eyes closed, even blasted like this. There's wasn't a moment when I didn't know where we were.

I pull the hat further down over my eyes.

'Cut left into Adams Street. Do it now while you got a chance.'

He doesn't argue. I hear the engine rev up, then we turn left and I feel us rumbling down Adams Street.

'Can't see no lane,' he mutters.

'It's just past the deli.'

'Can't see no deli,' says Xen.

'It's further down.'

She sparks back at me.

'How do you know if you ain't looking?'

'I don't need to look. I can tell.'

'You're weird.'

'You're shit.'

She makes a huffy noise but says no more. Nearby Bex gives a chuckle. I call out to Dig.

'You should be able to see the deli now.'

'I got it.'

'Be careful how you turn. It's narrow.'

Sound of the van slowing down. He's giving the wall of the deli a wide berth to get into the lane. And now we're heading down it. I can feel the rumble of the wheels over the uneven surface. We reach the end and I feel him turn into St Stephen's Gardens.

'You're right,' he says after a moment. 'We got round the police.'

Clever boy, Digsy. Only it won't last, Bigeyes. Cos there'll be more. And the porkers are the nicest of the nebs out cruising tonight. Run my hand under the woolly hat, up over my forehead. The bandage and the hat both feel wet. But I don't think I'm bleeding any more.

Just wish I had some energy, and my head straight again. But I got neither. Night's looking bleak, Bigeyes. Cos one thing's slick-sure: Dig's got no idea where to take me. He's rescued me—yeah, he's done that. Don't know why. Guilt probably, for hurting me, now he's worked out I didn't kill Trixi.

But he's brained out on what to do with me.

And he's starting to panic.

He's got porkers chewing his ankles, and grinks, and me blobbed in his van. And he's got a conscience cos he plugged me with his knife. Poor clapper. Cos I'll tell you, Bigeyes, you don't want a conscience. Not if you want to stay alive. So he's in the grime.

He's driving down St Stephen's Gardens and he's got no idea where to take me. Don't ask me how I know. There you go. We've reached the end of the road and he's stopped. I don't have to look out to see it. He's whipping his head to find a plan. But nothing's coming.

I call out again.

'Turn down Wisteria Drive, take the second right and the first left, and keep going till you reach the allotments.'

Another silence, just the engine grumbling. I can feel 'em all watching. They're scared of me now, Bigeyes. Trust me. I know. So I got to be careful. Scared means dangerous with some nebs. And these nebs were dangerous already.

They might have helped me. But that only counts for so much.

I keep my eyes closed, lie still. Darkness feels warm. Engine revs up again. Not a word from Dig, but he's doing what I said. Down Wisteria Drive, second right, first left, and we're on our way to the allotments.

'Follow the road round,' I say. 'Keep the allotments on your right.'

'Why don't you sit up?' says Xen. 'Sit up and watch proper.'

Hear that, Bigeyes? There's an edge in her voice. Sharper than it was before. I told you—she's scared. So she's dangerous again.

'I'm too tired to sit up,' I say.

'Which way now?' calls Dig.

'Right at the fork. Then right again. It'll take you—'

'I know where it takes me.' Dig gives a pause. 'I live in this city, OK?'

And there's an edge in Dig's voice too.

Got to watch my step, Bigeyes. Got to tread cute. They're not my friends. They're helping me for now but they're not my friends. I'm only here cos of Dig's conscience, but that's going to break soon. When it does, I'm smashed.

Close my eyes tight, try to think.

But it's hard. There's too much happening. And Dig's speeding up. I can hear it.

'Slow down,' I call.

'It's an empty road,' he answers.

'It's never an empty road.'

'What's that supposed to mean?'

'Never mind. Just slow down.'

He does, a bit. Not enough though. I know what's going on. He's losing his bottle. Yeah, Bigeyes, even Dig.

I got to stop this somehow.

'You got to slow down,' I say. 'Got to drive normal.'

'There's nobody in sight. We just left the houses behind. Who's to see us now?'

'You wouldn't want to know.'

He goes quiet, slows down a bit more. Still going too fast but it's better than it was. Stupid dimp. I owe him but he's a dimp. He's met some of the grinks already, seen what they can do. He's probably guessed one of 'em plugged his sister. He's got to keep his cool or we're finished.

He calls back again.

'Which way?'

'Just keep driving down Baltimore Road.'

He gives a kind of mutter, says no more. I got to watch this, Bigeyes. I'm drumming his brain big time and he doesn't like it. Better sit up. It's me lying down and knowing where we are that's blitzing his head. I push myself upright.

'Hey,' says Bex. 'You're meant to be lying down.'

I look at her. Don't know why but I don't hate her quite so much. She looks back. Something in her face I haven't seen before. Not what you'd call friendly. But not hostile either.

Can't say the same for Xen. She's twisted round in

the front seat and she's skimming me with her eyes.
I drill her back, keeping firm. She goes on watching
for a bit, then flicks an eye at Bex and leans close
to Dig.

'Digs?' she says.

'What?'

'He's sitting up.'

'I noticed.'

I catch Dig's glance in the mirror. Hard to tell if he's
relieved or angry. He's certainly scared. Not as much as
Xen but he's starting to choke up. I watch him in the
mirror. He's still checking me out but he doesn't want
to turn round proper.

'Another mile,' I say.

'Then what?'

'You'll see a crossroads with a pub called—'

'The Queen Anne,' he cuts in. 'I know it.'

'Go over the crossroads and there's a right turn
just after it.'

'And we go down there?'

Xen slants her eyes at him. She's been watching
me again but she's checking him out too. And there's
something in her face, Bigeyes, something that wasn't

there before. Don't know what it is. But she's looking at Dig different.

Looking at me different.

And then I get it. She's wondering where the power is. Cos she doesn't know any more, and it's cranking her out. She hates me already but if this goes on much longer, she'll start hating Dig too. Maybe she does already.

Dig speaks again.

'You ain't answered my question.'

'We don't turn right. We carry on. Past The Queen Anne, past the turning.'

'Then why mention the pub?' he says. 'Why mention the right turn?'

'Cos there's a little lane just past the turning.' I keep my voice steady. 'And you can miss it easy as sniff. So slow down when you get to the pub, and slow down again when you see the first right. The lane's just after it and it's tiny. If you don't watch close, you'll go past it.'

He says no more, just drives on. Xen goes on watching me for a bit, then turns away. I lie down again, eyes open now. Bex is sitting over me like before. Hard to read her face, but it's not angry. I know that much. She reaches out a hand.

'Don't touch me,' I say.

She pulls the hand back, turns her head away, murmurs.

'She keeps asking after you.'

'Who?' I say.

But I know the answer, Bigeyes. You bet I do. Bex turns back.

'You know who I mean.'

I picture Jaz's face. Christ, I wish she was here. I don't mean with all this shit. The danger, the dronks, all that. I mean her and me somewhere else. A little room in a little snug, pictures on the wall, mobiles hanging from the ceiling, toys, books. Yeah, books. Lots of 'em. I wish we had all that.

I could make her trust me again. Maybe even like me. I know I could. Bex goes on.

'You scared her so bad that time. But after she stopped screaming, she started asking where you were. And she's kept on.'

'Where's she now?'

'Somewhere safe.'

'Well, you keep her there, all right? You just bloody keep her there.'

Bex doesn't answer.

'Queen Anne ahead,' calls Dig.

I sit up again, peer forward.

'OK.' I reach out and point. 'See the right turn? Other side of the crossroads?'

'Yeah.'

'Head for it. But slow down when you get near. Cos the lane's just past it.'

He's still going too fast, Bigeyes, but I got no control over that. He'll drive how he wants. We rattle past the pub, over the crossroads and here's the right turn. Dig slows down at last, checking the side of the road.

'Can't see no lane,' he mutters.

'Bit further. You'll see some bushes and—'

'There!' says Bex.

She's moved forward and she's peering out with us. Xen glares at her for a moment, like she's guffed she didn't spot 'em herself. Bex takes no notice and points.

'There, Digs.'

'I got it.'

He checks round, turns into the lane. Leaves brush the van as we slip in.

'Bloody narrow,' he grumbles. Glances round at me. 'What is this place?'

'A private house.'

'You serious?'

'Yeah. Drive on till we're out of sight of the road. It's only a little way. Lane bends just ahead.'

He does as I say. I check behind, make sure we're cute.

'OK, stop.'

He stops, looks round. I check him over. And there it is again. Same thing in his face as Xen's got in hers. He's doing what she's doing. Wondering who's got the power. Cos he doesn't know any more. And he's scared it's not him.

He glances at Xen, Bex, me again. I got to play this smart, Bigeyes. Got to give him the power back somehow. Or make him think he's got it. Trouble is, he doesn't know what to do next. And I do. He scowls at me.

'What now?'

I nod to the left.

'Drive the van in among those trees.'

'Off the lane?'

'Yeah. Hide the van. Case someone cuts in after us.'

Like they could any moment, Bigeyes. Cos I'm telling you—that wasn't an empty road we just left behind. Dig might have thought it was but I know better. He turns off the lane, bumps the van over the grass and into the trees.

'Bit further,' I say.

'Shut your mouth.' He glowers at me. 'I'm doing it.'

He drives round the biggest clump of trees, stops, turns off the engine. Silence falls like a fog. They're all looking at me, waiting.

'Now what?' says Dig.

I look back at him and suddenly I can't speak. You know why, Bigeyes? Cos I'm choked up about this bit. Choked twice over. First up, there's too many nebs died cos of me. And second, I don't like showing people my snugs. Not even when I'm desperate.

Specially not Dig's kind of crew.

And this snug's special. Big old rambly house, set back down a twisty lane. Just one old gobbo in it, and he's away right now. I know that. I always check his desk diary when I'm there. Professor of Philosophy. Lectures all over the world. One busy gobbo.

And I like him. He's kind of helpless. He might know all the clever crap but he can't cook, can't sort his clothes, can't fix the fence, and he definitely can't work the burglar alarm. It was different when his wife was there. She cracked all that stuff for him. I couldn't use the snug much when she was around.

But she died last year. And since then I've felt sorry for him, cos he's sad. Yeah, I like him a lot. Not that he knows that. He doesn't even know I exist. But he's a sweet old gobbo and I don't want Dig's trolls crabbing all over his stuff. And worse still . . .

Worse by far . . .

I don't want the grinks locking on to him.

I couldn't bear that, Bigeyes. I'm telling you.

'Well?' says Dig.

I stare out the window. Just a short walk. That's all it is. A trig up the lane and there's a big, warm house waiting with no one in it. And he won't be back for a week.

I got to do it, Bigeyes. I got to rest so bad. And

somehow I got to trust these dronks. But all I can see in my head is the old prof's face peering at me. I peer back. He doesn't look happy. I don't suppose I do either.

I'm sorry, old gobbo. I'm really sorry.

His face doesn't change. I look back at Dig, and the trolls.

'Come with me,' I say.

Out the van, up the lane, round the back of the house. I'm still seeing that old prof's face in my head. Try to block it out, fix my rap on what I got to do. But it's hard. I'm so bombed out I'm hardly thinking.

Just know I got to get inside and rest.

And somehow try and stop these dregs grilling the old gobbo's house. Cos they will, Bigeyes. There's no way they'll leave it alone. This place won't be a snug after tonight. It's the last time I'll ever use it.

But I suppose I got no choice.

It's let 'em in or go somewhere else. And we got nowhere else as good as this right now. Nowhere I can think of anyway. And Dig's crew haven't come up with anything better.

'You sure about this?' says Dig.

I stop, look back at him. He's watching me in the darkness, eyes like bullets. Xen and Bex are standing either side of him, watching too. Watching me. I shrug.

'Yeah.'

'Nobody 'ere?' says Dig.

'It's empty.'

'There's a light on upstairs.'

There always is, Bigeyes. There'll be one on downstairs too, round the other side of the house. The lounge. The curtains'll be drawn and the radio'll be on. It's just the prof trying to tell the world he's in when he's out.

Bless him.

'It's empty,' I say.

I don't wait for an answer, just walk on round the building. Got to check things out like I always do, just in case I missed something. But it's all cute. Car's gone, garage empty. Upstairs light's the same it always is.

The landing light.

Walk further round. Close to the lounge window now.

'I can hear something,' says Xen. 'A radio.'

'There's no one in,' I say.

A hand grips my shoulder. It's Dig. I don't need to turn. But I do, slow. I stare into his eyes and there's that power thing again. He hates this, not knowing if he's in control. I got to tread soft, Bigeyes. I want to get inside, want to rest. But I got to work with this crew. I mustn't fizz 'em too much. Specially Dig.

He leans closer.

'How come you know about this place?'

I give another shrug.

'I know the guy who lives here. He's got his radio plugged into the wall socket by the television. And when he goes out, he leaves it on permanent. Keeps the curtains drawn and the light on.'

'What about that light upstairs?'

'It's the landing light. He leaves that on too.'

Dig's eyes move over me. I can almost feel 'em scratching me.

'You better be right,' he mutters.

I don't answer.

'So which way in?' he says. 'Break a window?'

Yeah, Bigeyes, like I'd do that. Even if I needed to. Which I don't. I shake my head.

'Much easier.'

I walk on, past the front door, still checking cute. I can feel 'em fuming up behind me. Like they don't know how important this is, watching, knowing, making sure. Yeah, the prof's out. I can feel that. Even blasted in my head I can feel that.

But I still check. I still make sure.

Cos I'm good.

'Now where are you going?' says Dig.

'Round the back of the house.'

'We just been there.'

Jesus, Bigeyes, see what I'm dealing with? I don't answer. Can't talk to this dronk. If he can't see why we got to check things thorough, I can't help him. Round to the back door, under the little porch, stop.

'Now what?' says Dig.

I look round. I was hoping I might be able to do this without 'em seeing. But it's no good. They're fixing me cute, all three. Reach up, feel round the inside of the porch, where the roof meets the side panel. And there it is.

The key.

Dig's watching, narrowed eyes.

'How'd you know he keeps it there?'

He doesn't keep it there, Bigeyes. This is a copy the prof doesn't know about. He keeps his own key under the plant pot over there. Yeah, Bigeyes, some nebs really are that stupid. This is one I made when I first started coming here. Case the old gobbo ever got wise enough to put the other one somewhere else.

'Never mind,' I say.

I open the door, let us in. Bex and Xen slip in ahead. Dig nods me through and comes after, then closes the door. From the lounge comes the sound of the radio. Xen and Bex look scared, like they're still not sure the house is empty.

'Come on,' I say.

I lead 'em through to the lounge, show 'em there's no one in there, then take 'em through the rest of the house. But I'm hating this, Bigeyes. When I'm here on my own, it's OK. I treat the place good, like I do all my snugs.

And I like this one. I always did. I like the photos everywhere, of him and his wife. All the awards he's won, and the ornaments in the cabinets. And the books. Yeah, the books. He must have thousands.

Big stuff too, heavy stuff. Philosophy and all. Can't crack most of it. But I like reading it. Don't know why. Maybe it was that Nietzsche book I told you about. The one I read in that other snug. Maybe that's what did it.

I kind of like this stuff now. Doesn't beat stories. Nothing could. But it stings my head and I'm cute about that. Yeah, I like this snug. But not with Dig and the trolls here. With them around I feel like I'm pissing on the old man's face.

And when the rest of the crew get here, it'll be worse. Cos they're on their way, Bigeyes. Trust me. Xen's on her mobile already, talking to Riff. She sees me watching and takes off to another room.

'I'll check if there's any food,' says Bex.

And she goes.

I look at Dig. We're standing in the hall again and he's close. He's been like that all the time we were going through the rooms. I check out his eyes. They're hard like before, hard and wary. He's still got his conscience. But only just.

He nods me towards the lounge.

I walk through ahead of him, throw myself down on the sofa. I just want to curl up and sleep. I'm not ready to talk, not yet. I want to rest first, think first. But Dig's got stuff in his head. There'll be no rest till we've sorted that.

He leans down, turns off the radio, sits in the armchair, pulls it closer. Xen comes back. She's stopped talking on the phone but she's texting someone. Sits on the floor, glances at me, then at Dig. His face doesn't change. She goes back to her texting. Bex appears in the doorway.

'No food. Nothing.'

I could have told her that, Bigeyes. You know why? Cos there's never any food in the house now. The old prof's fallen apart since his missus died. That's another reason why I feel sorry for him. He used to eat real good when she was around.

And so did I.

'Make some tea,' says Dig. 'There's got to be some of that.'

'There ain't,' says Bex. 'Instant coffee, that's all. No milk.'

'Then make that, for Christ's sake.' Dig glares at her. 'And when we got our coffee . . . ' He fixes his gaze back on me. 'We'll decide what we're going to do about Blade.'

There's a silence. Just the sound of Xen texting. Then that stops. I stare back at Dig. I got to play this right.

'There's nothing you got to do about me,' I say.

He doesn't answer, just watches. Xen jets a glance at him, but he doesn't notice. He's still watching my face. I'm watching both of 'em. And Bex, still standing in the doorway.

'There's nothing you got to do about me,' I say. 'I just got to rest. And then we can split.'

Dig shakes his head.

'We ain't going to split just yet.'

'Why not?'

'Cos you got stuff to explain.'

'Yeah?'

'Yeah.'

I watch him. He watches me.

'Like what?' I say eventually.

He leans closer.

'Well, for starters,' he says, 'you can tell us about them marks on your back.'

It's taken 'em long enough to ask. The trolls would have seen the marks that time they stripped me on the towpath. But nobody spoke up. Not even Bex. And she had plenty of chances later.

So did you, Bigeyes.

But maybe you were all scared. Cos wounds freak people out. Specially wounds like mine.

'Well?' says Dig.

I'm not telling him, Bigeyes. Or you. Forget it, OK? It's like I said right in the beginning—I choose what I say and what I don't. You can choose whether to stay or wig it somewhere else.

My secret.

Not yours.

'I'm waiting,' says Dig.

He's watching cute. So's Xen. So's Bex. She still hasn't moved from the doorway. I glance at her.

'Thought you were making coffee.'

'Don't change the subject,' says Dig.

I look back at him.

'I'm not,' I say. 'The subject's coffee. When that's here, we'll talk.'

I hold his eyes, drill him. He doesn't like this. He's not used to it. Maybe he can see something I once was, something that's still left from the past. Maybe he doesn't know it's gone. And that's fine by me. I need him like this. Moment he knows he's stronger than me, I'm done.

He drills me back, hard as he can, but it's no good. He wavers first. Tries to cover it by flicking his gaze at Bex.

'Coffee,' he snaps. 'Make it quick.'

She goes. And we wait.

Silence. A long silence. Just the sound of the kettle heating up in the kitchen and Bex hunting for cups. Dig and Xen watch. And I watch back. And we go on waiting. Bex comes back eventually, holding a tray with four cups on it.

'I found some sugar,' she says.

'Nobody wants any,' says Dig.

She doesn't answer, just puts the tray down. Nobody moves. She glances round, takes a cup in each hand, holds 'em out to Dig and Xen. Neither take any notice.

'I'll have one,' I say.

She holds one of the cups out for me. I take it and put it on the floor. She keeps the other one herself and slumps with it in the chair by the television. The other two cups sit on the tray, untouched.

'I'm waiting,' says Dig.

I shake my head.

'You first.'

'About what?'

'About everything.'

He reaches out, picks up a cup of coffee, blows off the steam.

'Everything's a lot of things,' he drawls.

'You better get started then.'

He watches me over the rim of the cup. I wait. He'll talk first. He's holding out long as he can but he'll talk first. Don't ask me how I know. He takes a sip, then suddenly starts.

'We thought you killed Trixi. Or Bex killed her. Or you both did. Specially when the girls saw you trying to get Jaz away. Police turned up, asking questions.

Tammy told 'em all about you. I didn't want her to. I wanted you for myself.'

I reach up, feel the wound in my head. It's hurting again. But it's dry.

Dig watches, goes on.

'So when them other guys showed up, it seemed like a better option.'

'Paddy,' I say quietly.

'Yeah.' Dig takes another sip of coffee. 'And his mates.'

I shake my head. 'And you believed 'em.'

'I still believe 'em.'

'What?'

'I still believe 'em.' Dig gives a little smile, but it quickly goes. 'Not about you killing Trixi like they said. I did then but I don't now. But I believe 'em about the other stuff.'

'What other stuff?'

'About you being a killer.'

I feel Xen stiffen on the floor.

'Cos you are,' says Dig. 'Ain't you?'

I don't answer. He waits, like to give me space. I say nothing, let him fill it instead.

'I was happy to believe Paddy,' he goes on. 'So when he said him and his mates was after you for other murders, it seemed like a good idea to work together. Riff kept in touch with 'em. And one way and another, we found you.'

'Yeah.' I feel my wound again. 'You found me.'

He says nothing. He's watching close, not my eyes this time, but my hand on the bandage. And I can see it in his face, Bigeyes, bung-clear. He's stopped caring. No messing. Conscience is wiped now.

'So what changed everything?' I say.

'We threw you out the *Sally Rose* and kicked Bex out an' all, cos we didn't want her no more. She can tell you the next bit.'

I look at Bex. She's like Xen, sitting rigid.

'I saw them guys,' she says. 'They was following you to the warehouse. And then I saw this old woman. I recognized her from the bungalow. But I was too freaked out to think much. I just told her we got to do something. But then I panicked and ran off.'

Xen gives a snort. Dig rounds on her.

'Don't assume you'd have done no better.'

'I would have.'

'I don't think so.'

She gives him a baleful stare. He takes no notice, gives Bex a nod.

'Get on with it.'

Bex looks at me.

'I was running off,' she says, 'running like shit. I'm way down the path and then I hear these gunshots. Two of 'em. Bang! Bang! Scared the crap out of me. I wanted to run on but I stopped and hid. There was this upturned dinghy just off the path. Wreck of a thing. I crouched down behind that. And I'm crying cos I think you're dead. And then . . . I know I got to go back. Find out what's happened. Do something. So I starts to run back—'

'See?' Dig swivels back to Xen. 'You wouldn't have done that.'

'I would.'

'You wouldn't. You'd have pissed off out of it.'

Xen doesn't answer, just scowls. This is bad, Bigeyes. I'm telling you. He doesn't need to whip Xen over like this. She's angry enough already. He'll only make it worse. But there's nothing I can do about it. This is about the three of 'em. And I'm not part of that.

He's looking back at me now.

'So Bex gets back where she was,' he says, 'and finds the police hanging around, and an ambulance taking you off to hospital. Comes back to the *Sally Rose* and tells us what's happened. And next day we hear about Paddy.'

'Being caught?' I say.

Dig shakes his head.

'Being dead.'

Shit, Bigeyes, he's smacked me cold with this one. I knew about the porkers getting Paddy. The grunt told me when I was lying outside the warehouse. But I didn't see this coming.

Dig drinks the rest of his coffee, puts down the cup.

'It was on the news,' he goes on. 'About this guy being taken in by the police. Nothing about his name but it was obvious from the details they meant Paddy. And they was going on about how there was forensic evidence linking him and Trixi. Enough to know he was in the bungalow. Enough to know it wasn't you or Bex done my sister.'

He glances at Xen.

'Enough for me anyway,' he adds.

She turns her head away.

'But how'd he die?' I say.

Dig looks back at me.

'Result of a previous injury, the news said. Seems someone hit him with a cricket bat. Don't ask me how they knew it was a cricket bat. I don't suppose Paddy told 'em. But who cares? They got the forensic evidence. So I knew it wasn't you killed Trix.'

He watches me, hard.

'Must have whopped Paddy real good,' he murmurs. 'Whoever had that cricket bat.'

I don't answer. He waits a bit longer but I stay quiet. He goes on, still watching.

'So there's me starting to feel bad about what I done to your head. But I ain't got no time to think cos suddenly you gone missing again. It's all over the bloody news. You've broken out the hospital and there's been more murders. And now we're in the shit too.'

He leans closer.

'Cos the police is back asking stuff. And more of them guys. Not Paddy's crew. Other guys, guys we

never seen before. Smooth bastards. Never come
when the police is there, always some other time.
Checking me out, checking the girls, checking Riff. Every
time we look round, there's someone hanging close.'

He pulls out the big knife, looks it over.

'They ain't never no trouble. It's all matey-matey.
How's it going, Dig? All right, Dig? Seen that boy anywhere, Dig? Keep in touch, mate.' Dig sniffs. 'But I'm
not stupid. So me and Riff and the girls talk. We agree
to take Bex back . . . ' He throws another glance at
Xen, then fixes me again. 'And help you.'

Yeah, right. Hear that, Bigeyes? He almost spat out
the last bit. Like he couldn't bear to say it. But I guess
I can't be choosy. Fact is I'm here cos he went and got
me. He didn't have to like it. He just had to do it. And
he did. So I should be grateful.

Can't quite work out why I'm not.

Maybe it's cos I know that whatever he's done, he
still hates me as much as I hate him. In which case, the
sooner this game's over, the better for both of us. No
more pretend. I watch him for a moment, wait for him
to speak. He's got more to say. Not much, but I want
to hear it.

'So we goes looking for you,' he says. 'Some mate of Trixi's tells us he's seen you on the north side. Says you was riding a bike. Riff takes the van that way while I check out other places on the motorbike. No sign. Then we gets another message. Someone Sash knows thinks he saw you. So we goes on looking.'

Dig glances down, fingers the knife.

'Only there's others looking too.'

Glances up again, straight at me.

'You know who I mean.'

Yeah, Bigeyes, I know who he means. And he's not talking about the porkers. I'm thinking back to the lane. The dark little lane and my dark little dream of safety. How dimpy was that, Bigeyes? Eh? Must have been off my head to think I could get away. I'm seeing 'em again now, the figures crowding round in the night.

But I'm still alive. And I'm here. Cos of this guy in front of me. Whatever else I think of him, I owe him.

'Thanks,' I say.

Dig looks at me quizzical.

'For helping me,' I add.

He gives a sort of laugh.

'Long time coming,' he mutters. He fingers the knife again. 'But if you mean it, I'll take it.'

'I mean it.'

He glances at Bex, Xen, Bex again. I check out the trolls. Xen's looking down, meeting nobody's eyes, body all tight. Bex looks wary—of Xen, me, Dig, everything. Dig fixes me again.

'So I got you away and we put you on the motorboat. Didn't know what else to do. Couldn't use none of our places cos them guys keep showing up, and the police. So we thought of the boat. But then we saw 'em checking out the moorings in that launch. So we come and got you. And now we're here.'

'Thanks,' I say again.

We watch each other in silence. I wait for Dig to break it.

'So,' he says, 'them marks on your back . . . '

'What about 'em?'

'Going to show me?'

'No.'

His face hardens.

'The girls told me they was pretty spectacular.'

'So?'

'So I reckon you owe me a look.'

'I don't owe anyone a look.'

His eyes run over me. I'm watching him cute, Bigeyes. Yeah, I know. You're thinking show him and have done. But that's cos you want to look at 'em too, right? Well, you can't, and he can't. I don't care what I owe him.

He's not seeing 'em. Unless he forces me. And he might try. He might just try. He leans back, stroking the knife, then speaks, low voice.

'So what do you owe me?'

'I said thanks.'

'That's it? Thanks?'

'Yeah.'

'Blade,' says Bex.

I glance at her. She's got a pleading look in her face. Never seen it there before. Makes her look vulnerable. Don't know what I feel. She speaks again.

'You got to tell us about them guys. Who they is.'

'You don't want to know 'em.'

'How come they're after you? What you done to 'em?'

Nothing, Bigeyes. Before you ask. They're not the

ones I've hurt. It's the nebs who've sent 'em that's the problem. They're the ones who really want me.

'I can't tell you about 'em,' I say. 'I got some ene-mies, OK?'

'More than some,' says Dig. 'I saw 'em crowding round you.'

'And there's more coming.' I fix my eyes on him. 'Listen. You don't want to make this your problem. You've helped me. I'm grateful. But let it go. And let me go.'

Dig looks down at the knife, runs a finger along the blade.

'And where will you go?' He looks up. 'Eh? Going to tell me that much?'

'Away,' I answer. 'Somewhere far, somewhere safe.'

'Is there such a place?'

I don't answer. Cos I don't know.

Dig puts the knife away. Xen's mobile starts to ring. She pulls it out.

'Yeah?'

We watch her in silence, waiting.

'It's a little lane,' she says. 'Bushes and stuff. You got it? OK.'

She rings off, looks round at us.

'They're 'ere.'

Xen goes to the front door to let 'em in. Riff comes first, eyes darting. What a surprise. I'll tell you what he's doing, Bigeyes. And I'll tell you what he's not doing. He's not checking for trouble. He's checking to see what he can cream.

I got that old prof's face in my head again. I'm sorry, old gobbo. I didn't want to bring these dregs into your house. But I just didn't know what else to do. Please don't be angry with me.

Kat and Tammy come next, then Sash.

Carrying Jaz in her arms.

'Jesus!' says Dig. 'What you bring the kid for?'

'She won't sleep without Bex,' says Sash.

'You was meant to stay behind and look after her. Not bring her here.'

Tammy thrusts her face in front of Dig's.

'You deaf or something? Sash just said. Jaz won't sleep without Bex. And you know it. We found that out Day One, remember?'

Dig doesn't answer. Jaz starts to whimper, reaches for Bex. I feel kind of weird, Bigeyes. Maybe it's cos I want her to reach for me. But she hasn't even looked at me. She's just staring at Bex.

'Put her down,' says Bex. 'She's knackered.'

'Ain't slept, that's why,' says Sash.

'Then put her down.'

Sash puts Jaz down. Bex gives a smile.

'Come here, Fairybell.'

Jaz runs into her arms, buries her face.

'There you go,' says Bex, stroking her head. 'All right now.'

Jaz goes on whimpering. I look round at the others. They're all watching Dig.

'So what's going on?' says Riff.

'Me and Blade have had a little talk,' says Dig.

He glances at Xen and Bex. Bex doesn't notice. She's snuggling Jaz, kissing the girl's hair. Xen just looks away. Dig watches her for a moment, then turns back to face me.

'We've had a little talk,' he goes on. 'Only I done most of the talking. Blade here don't choose to say much.'

He drills me with his eyes.

'But I reckon we're quits now. Him and me.'

He's waiting, Bigeyes. Waiting for something back. Fair enough. Can't argue with that. He slashed my head. But he got me away from the grinks. I give him a nod, a small one. But he sees it.

'So what you brung us 'ere for?' says Tammy.

Dig turns to her.

'To get Blade away.'

'You what?'

'To get him away.'

'What for?' Tammy stares at him. 'We done enough for this shithead, ain't we?'

'No, we ain't.'

'Why not?'

'Cos I say so.' Dig fixes her hard for a moment. 'We got him this far. We're going to finish it proper. Nice and tidy. So listen. We rest for a few hours. Cos we're all tired. And just before dawn we drive him out the city.'

'I don't like it,' says Tammy.

'Nor me,' says Sash.

'Well, I don't care,' says Dig. 'That's what we're doing.'

'But them guys is all over the place,' says Sash. 'And the police.'

'It's just to get him away.' Dig pauses. 'We go at the quiet time, just before dawn. Two vans, five minutes apart, different routes. One as a decoy. The other one to get him out the city. I'll take that one. Drop him where he wants and that's it. All done.'

He glances at me. And I nod again.

Yeah, that's it. All done.

For you lot anyway.

There's no more argument, even from Tammy. But she's not happy. I can tell. Nor are the others. They look blown out. And you can't blame 'em, Bigeyes. There's that many grinks in the city now, it's dangerous for everybody.

Dig checks his watch.

'Half past midnight. Rest up for a few hours. I'll call you when we're leaving.'

We split. Or rather they do. I'm staying on the sofa. No point moving. I won't sleep anyway. I'm bombed out but I know I won't sleep, not while I'm still here.

I got to get out of the city, Bigeyes. Maybe then I'll sleep. But first I got to find a new place and play dead all over again. And play it better this time. Make sure the grinks don't find me.

And somehow stop Dig and his crew getting hurt too. Cos I don't want that to happen. They've helped me, Bigeyes. I don't like 'em, and they don't like me, but they've kept me alive and I owe 'em. And there's something even more important. Much more.

Jaz.

I got to keep her safe at all costs.

Check her out, Bigeyes. She's falling asleep in Bex's arms. Hasn't glanced at me once since she came in. Just went straight for Bex. I guess that's fair. Long as the kid's OK, doesn't matter what I feel.

Except to me.

It matters to me.

Dig's still sitting in the armchair. Xen's wigged it upstairs, so have Tammy and Sash. I can hear 'em moving about. I feel guilty for the old prof again. I hate the thought of these dronks tramping over his gear.

Riff and Kat are still hanging about. Kat's blasted and wants to sleep. Anyone can see that. But Riff's still picking stuff up, checking it over.

'Riff,' says Dig. 'We got to sleep.'

Riff looks round at him, then at Kat. Puts down the little vase he was holding, gives her a wink.

'Come on, then,' he smirks.

Yeah, dungpot, we know what you want. But he's out of luck, Bigeyes. Cop a glint at Kat's face. See that? It's a big, big no. She sees me looking, gives a flinty little smile, walks out the room and up the stairs. Riff follows, checking ornaments as he goes.

'Blade.'

Dig's watching me again.

'Yeah?' I say.

'Me and Bex on the sofa.'

It's not a request. I can hear it in his voice. And you know what, Bigeyes? I don't give two bells. He wants his power back. Well, he can have it. He's helping me one last time. I owe him the sofa. I stand up, look over at Bex.

She's stood up too, holding Jaz in her arms, fast asleep now. She carries the kid over, sits down with her on the sofa. Dig comes over too, sits down in my place.

'You don't got to go, Blade,' says Bex. 'Have Dig's armchair.'

Yeah, Bigeyes. Cute thought, eh? I don't even have to look at Dig's face to know how much he likes the idea. Well, he'll have to deal with it. I'm sitting in the armchair. Not cos I want to give 'em trouble. But cos . . . well . . . if you really want to know . . .

I want to be near Jaz.

I don't want to let her out of my sight. Cos this is the last night I'll ever see her. And I want as much of her as I can get, even asleep. Cos you know what? I'm going to have to live off that memory soon.

Slump down in the armchair, close my eyes.

Someone turns off the light. I don't bother to check who. Dig probably. When I peep out again, it's all dark. Dig and Bex are curled up on the sofa, Jaz nestled under Bex's arm. They look kind of sweet. Can't say they don't.

And I feel weird again.

But then somehow I sleep. Didn't expect to but it comes over me like warm rain. And a dream comes with it. I'm dreaming of Becky, sweet Becky who died. I can see her face clear as the sun. And she's talking to me.

Only I can't make out the words.

Then I get 'em.

'Blade,' she's murmuring.

And that's it. My name.

'Blade, Blade . . .'

That's all she's saying. And now there's a hand on my shoulder, and it's rocking me gentle. And the name's coming again.

'Blade, Blade.'

And that's gentle too. So I open my eyes. And here's the room back again, and it's dark like before. Rex and Dig have left the sofa but I know where they've gone. I can hear 'em upstairs. In the old prof's bedroom. The one he shared with his wife.

The hand rocks my shoulder again. The voice repeats my name.

'Blade,' it says.

'Jaz,' I answer.

And she climbs up into my arms and I hold her tight.

She doesn't talk. But she's awake, she's aware of me. She's looking up at me with sleepy eyes. I look down into 'em, try and smile. Don't know if I manage it. But I speak. I manage that, just.

'All right, baby?'

I sound like a dimp. I'm embarrassed by my own voice. She doesn't answer. Closes her eyes, opens 'em again. She's only half-awake. I pull her closer. She doesn't resist. And nor do I. Didn't know I could hold someone close and not feel bad.

But I'm cute about this. Touching, being touched. Cos she's touching me too. Her little hand's moving, just a bit, over my arm. Stops, moves, stops. Now it's resting, still on my arm. She wriggles a bit, closes her eyes again.

More sounds upstairs. Not loud but enough for me to clap 'em. Just hope Jaz can't. They're not the sounds a kid should hear. But it's OK. I think she's dropping off again. I'm wrong.

'Blade,' she murmurs.

I look down at her. She's peering up at me again, same sleepy eyes. I lean closer, whisper.

'Do you want to hear a story?'

She gives a little moan. I think that's a yes.

'It's a great story,' I say. 'About this little girl.'

'What's she called?'

'Jaz.'

'That's my name.'

'I know, baby. Weird, yeah?'

'Hm.'

'Do you want to know what happens to her?'

'Hm.'

'She's sitting by this rabbit hole one day and guess who she sees coming along?'

'Bunny.'

'Yeah, it's Mr Bunny.'

'Where's he going?'

'He's just coming back from the shops.'

'Where's Mrs Bunny?'

'She's down the bunny hole. She's angry with him.'

'What for?'

'Cos he's late. She sent him out ages ago to get some bread but he met a friend in the shop and that was it. No getting away for hours.'

'Why?'

'Cos he's a chatterbox.'

'Mr Bunny?'

'Yeah. Yak yak yak. Talks for ever.'

Jaz's eyes widen.

'For ever?'

'Well, he stops sometimes to have a rest. But pretty soon he starts all over again.'

'Is Mrs Bunny very angry with him?'

'Very very very angry. And she's going to be even more angry when he gets back inside the bunny hole.'

'Why?'

'Cos he forgot the bread.'

'Where is it?'

'He left it back in the shop. But don't worry, cos Jaz comes to the rescue.'

Her eyes are closing again. More sounds upstairs. But they're easing off a bit. And now it's all quiet. Just the sound of Jaz breathing, tucked into my chest. She looks so beautiful, Bigeyes, like a little flower. Makes me think of Becky again.

'You asleep, baby?' I murmur.

No answer. The breathing goes on. I stare round the room, whisper into the darkness.

'Too many stories, Jaz. Too many to tell. And they all seem to hurt.'

I look down at her again.

'But I'll make sure yours has got a happy ending.'
I stroke her hair. 'I'll finish it when you wake up.'

She goes on sleeping. I'm glad. I want her to sleep.
Even if I can't. I breathe out, listen. House is quiet now.
Not a sound anywhere. Even Jaz's breathing's gone
silent. Check round. Behind me's the old prof's radio
and next to it the little lights of the electric clock.

Five past two.

I reach out, switch the radio on, volume down as
low as I can manage. Out comes a voice, faint but
clear: some newsy woman.

' . . . but the boy is still at large. There have been
unconfirmed reports of him in different parts of the
city, including one alleged sighting close to the house
in which Mrs Turner was murdered. The area has been
cordoned off and police are appealing for witnesses . . . '

I look down at Jaz again. No change. Eyes closed,
body still. She's sleeping deeper than ever. The newsy
woman's voice goes on but I'm not really listening. I
know what the porkers know, and what they don't.
But then I hear something—and stiffen.

' . . . an elderly woman, calling herself Lily . . . '

Christ, Bigeyes. They're talking about Mary.

Another voice, some gobbo reporter.

'Not really, Joanna. At this stage the police are simply saying they're anxious to interview the lady. She apparently found the boy when he was lying injured outside the warehouse, accompanied him to the hospital and spoke to him when he came round after his operation. She's not been seen since and though the police took a statement from her at the time of the injury, it now appears that she gave a false name and address. To complicate matters further, a witness has come forward and reported seeing someone matching this woman's description close to the bungalow where the teenager Trixi Kenton was killed.'

I turn off the radio. And darkness fills my head.

What's happened to me, Bigeyes? Has my brain stopped working? Why wasn't I ready for this? Cos I've been thinking of Jaz and only Jaz, that's why. Wanting her to be all right. And that's cute. That's how it should be. But what about Mary?

Why didn't I look out for her?

Do you crack what I'm saying? This is bad, Bigeyes. I should have told her to get away. She can't stay here,

not in this city. The porkers want her but they're not
the grime. Even if they find her, they won't be able to
protect her. The grinks'll want her more.

They've met her twice already. The old girl with the
gun. They'll know all about that. So why's she still
alive? Cos maybe they didn't connect her first go. They
maybe just thought here's some old bird with a bit of
spit and she's looking out for some kid.

And that's how it was.

Only now the porkers have blown that open. It's
news. Everything about that report says Mary
are linked up. Everything about it says she
w something. The porkers want to talk to

ks'll want to talk to her even more.

shit here, Bigeyes. And she doesn't
get out of the city, tonight, in the
ground big time, then wig it when she
before they find her.

I might be too late already.

Check the clock again. Nearly quarter past two. I
ot a couple of hours before Dig cranks us up. Can't
ng Mary from here. That'll get the nebs at the pub

involved. I got to tell her—and just her. And I got to do it now.

I look down at Jaz. Still sleeping in my arms. Beautiful girl.

'Beautiful girl,' I whisper.

I ease up from the chair, keeping her tight. She shifts a bit, wriggles in my arms, settles again. I carry her over to the sofa, put her softly down, cushion under her head. She goes on sleeping.

Like she could for ever.

I kneel down, move close again.

'Don't wake up, baby,' I murmur.

She doesn't. She just lies there, in the the darkness.

'I'll come back for you,' I whispe will. I know I left you once before back. But I will this time. No ma I'll come back and finish your story. A bye.'

I stand up again. But I'm still looking down. I can take my eyes from her, Bigeyes. I can't do it. But I go to. Got to make myself. For Mary's sake. I reach out hand. I want to touch her again. Once more. Just little touch. But she moves, turns over, pushes her face into the cushion.

And I pull my hand back.

It's now, Bigeyes. It's got to be now.

And I head for the door.

Into the hall, soft, slow, listening cute. No sound anywhere in the house. Nothing from the old prof's bedroom. Nothing from anywhere else. I could be in an empty snug.

Stop at the back door, listen again.

Still quiet. Just hope they're all sleeping, but I don't know if I'll be that lucky. I wouldn't sleep if I was them. Not if I knew what's sniffing after us. Push open the back door, slip out, close it soft.

Tiny click but not much. Listen again, then round the side of the house, down the lane, off into the trees. Two vans parked together. And here's the good news.

No fuss over keys. Dig left his in the ignition. Didn't think I spotted that, did you, Bigeyes? Well, I did. I saw him. Stupid tick. He thinks we're all comfy here, off the road, out of sight. So he didn't bother with the keys.

Bad news is the van's only got a drip of petrol.

I spotted that too.

Riff's motor's probably got more but I'm not sneaking round the house trying to cream the keys off him. So we're taking Dig's van. Let's just hope the engine doesn't wake everybody up.

Jump in, close the door, check the petrol gauge.

See what I mean? Quarter tank. He should have juiced up before the crap flew, but there you go. That's his business. Just got to pray we get there and back. I got no money to buy petrol and wouldn't dare stop at a garage if I had.

Let's get this over with.

Check round, turn the key. Engine fires straight off. Let it tick over till it chums up. I'm not revving loud case they hear. Check over there, Bigeyes, through the trees. You can just see part of the house. Any lights going on?

I can't see any.

Let's go.

Reverse gear, back to the apple tree, twist round, into the lane, down to the road. Stop, check both ways. No headlights either side, nothing in my mirror from the direction of the house. I'm half-expecting Dig and the others to come running.

But they're not. I think we've done it, Bigeyes. They're sleeping on. I hope they don't stop. They're safer sleeping. Safer for everyone, including themselves. Come on. We got to move.

Left into the road and off. Getting really scared now, Bigeyes. I tell you, I'm hating this—heading back into the city. Cos that's where the grinks are. Or most of 'em. They'll be out this way too but the city'll be crawling with 'em.

Least we're heading for South Street. It's not far off the centre but it's kind of a quiet little road and I might just be able to park out of sight and slip down to The Crown without anyone noticing.

I've already thought of a way into the pub.

That's where knowing the city helps. But let's get there first. If the porkers or grinks spot me driving the van, we won't even make it to The Crown. And we're starting to pick up traffic now.

Slow traffic.

Scary traffic.

Who drives anywhere this time of the morning?

Sleepy nebs, drunken nebs, that's what you're thinking. Nebs going home, nebs going away. And you'd be
right. But I don't see any of 'em. I just see danger.

In every car.

More traffic, porkers now, two cars and a motorbike coming the other way. They slip past. Drive on,
check the mirror. They haven't stopped. Left into
Western Avenue, down to the end, right into Sion Way.

More porkers, a van this time, parked just ahead,
same side of the road. Got to drive past it, no way out.
Some policeman standing on the pavement, talking to
a gobbo.

But it's the gobbo in trouble, not me. He's waving
his arms about, yelling. Policeman doesn't look fazed.
But he doesn't check me out either. Drive on past, turn
down Madeira Drive. And now it gets interesting.

Two more cars, and they're not porkers. Don't
know why they bother me. They're just cars in front,
heading the same way as me. Nobody staring back. So
why'm I getting spun? Never mind, Bigeyes. I just am.
I got a nose for grinks.

Nearest car turns left. I carry on. Other car's still in
front of me. Three big gobbos crowded in the back,

two more in the front. Can't make out their faces. Could be anyone. Guys cruising home from a night out. But I'm getting choked wondering.

They turn off too and I drive past.

Over the traffic lights, down past the bus station. I'm going the long way round, Bigeyes, missing out the one-way system. I want to come to South Street from behind the football stadium. It's a bit dronky cos there's lots of duffs round those streets but it's more deserted and I'd rather meet a duff than a grink.

Here we go. Into Cornwall Drive, round the round-about, straight over, down Schubert Avenue. Van's rattling a bit but the petrol's holding up. I've been watching the gauge, even if you haven't.

End of the road, stop, check. Left at the junction, and now we keep straight on, follow the road round. See the stadium on the right? Big dusky thing, all quiet now. Don't like this place much. Only ever come here on match days to lift wallets.

Or I used to.

Cos that's over, Bigeyes. In this city anyway.

I'm thinking of Mary now. I'm starting to see her face in my mind. I've been pushing it aside all the way here cos I was worried I might not even make it to the pub. But now we're almost there. And I'm scared in case something happens at the last minute.

Or I mess up.

But here's South Street straight ahead.

Turn off just before. We'll take this spitty little side street. It's a bit rough and narrow but we can park the van down it and come at the pub from the back. Keep off South Street altogether. Van doesn't like the pot-holes but we're almost there now.

Pull over, engine off, check round.

High walls, high buildings. Old houses, Bigeyes, built long before the stadium. And The Crown's ancient. They probably put that thing up before foot-ball got invented.

Out of the van, check round again.

Nobody in sight, thank Christ. There's usually some old duff slapping it under a blanket. No sign of anyone here. OK, Bigeyes. Check out the wall on your left. That's the back of The Crown. The crumbly building beyond it's the pub.

Told you it was ancient. And the great thing about ancient buildings is they're a jink to break into.

Come on, let's go find Mary. We got to get this thing sorted.

Over the wall, whack of a climb, drop down the other side. Got to tread cute now. Never been in here before. Long garden with tables and chairs, most of 'em covered up. Creep to the back door, check it over.

Easy piss, Bigeyes. Door's got a lock even you could pick. But if the drainpipe's firm, we can climb in through that upstairs window they've so kindly left open for us. Should take us straight to the bedrooms too and we won't have to fumble about on the stairs.

Drainpipe's cute. Up we go, slow, slow. I'm trying to go steady but I'm desperate to see Mary now, desperate to talk to her. I'm nervous too, Bigeyes. I don't mind admitting. I'm nervous cos I'm remembering what she said to me last time we spoke.

Here's the window. Just ajar but no problem. Ease it up, nice and quiet, slide in. Bathroom, dim, cold floor, tap dripping into the basin. Reach out, turn it off, check the door. It's half-open.

Step through. Landing stretching right and left, doors all along it. Now it gets hard, Bigeyes. Cos I got no idea which one she's in. I could wake up some other neb. And waking Mary could be bad too. If I scare her, she'll scream.

Got to choose, left or right?

Left.

We'll check out the rooms closest to South Street first. Creep down, listening, listening. Car roars past the pub, doesn't stop, sound recedes. First door, closed. Doesn't feel right. Can't explain it. But Mary's not in there.

Don't ask me how I know.

Next door, next door, next door. I'm not even trying 'em, Bigeyes. They don't feel right. You're thinking this is crazy. Maybe it is. But she's not in those rooms, OK? She's just not in 'em. She's . . .

Ssssh! Listen.

Snoring.

Room at the end. Must be overlooking the street. And someone's in there. Least we know they're asleep. Tiptoe down, slow, slow, and I'm getting this feeling, Bigeyes.

Yeah, I know. Could be anyone. And you may be right. But I got to check. I got to do it. Walk up to the door, reach out, touch the handle, squeeze, turn. Sound of snoring stops.

I wait, take a breath, push open the door.
And see Mary's eyes staring at me.

She's in an old single bed, propped up with pillows so she's almost upright. Hair's hanging loose over a dronky nightdress, torn in one sleeve. She's got her day-clothes thrown over a chair. Poky little room: rickety furniture, scuffy carpet.

She looks ill.

'You look ill,' she says.

I give a start. Wasn't expecting her to say that.

'Close the door,' she says.

I close the door, slow, quiet. Stand there, watching her. She's running her eyes over me. Doesn't look startled at all. It's almost like she was expecting me.

'I was expecting you,' she says.

She's freaking me out, talking like this.

'You're in danger,' I mutter.

She still doesn't look startled. Seems almost amused. Then her face softens.

'Come over here,' she says.

I walk up to the bed. Her eyes are watching me

close now. I remember how they did that in the bunga-low, when she was scared I might hurt her. I hope she's not scared now. I don't want her to be scared of me.

'I'm not scared of you,' she says.

Jesus, Bigeyes. I wish she'd stop gobbing what's in my head. It's spooking me bad. I sit down on the bed, out of reach.

'No,' she says.

'No what?'

'You've got to get over this.'

'Over what?'

'Being touched by a friend who means you no harm.'

I don't answer, just sit there, feeling trapped. She holds out a hand. I can see it's an effort for her to lift it. I stay where I am.

'Come on,' she murmurs. 'Sit closer.'

I move closer, just a bit. She drops her hand to the bed, gives a sigh.

'I can't hold the damn thing up in the air for ever.' She gives a chuckle, then turns and stretches over the other side of the bed. Pokes about a bit, like she's look-ing for something, then straightens up, holding a gun.

Points it at me.

'Now sit closer.'

I shake my head.

'You told me it's only got blanks in it.'

'Oh, damn.' She clicks her tongue. 'I did, didn't I?'

I can't help it, Bigeyes. I just love that Irish voice. It's like she's singing rather than talking. I mimic it back to her.

'Yeah, you did.'

She raises an eyebrow.

'Please tell me that wasn't meant to be an Irish accent.'

She puts down the gun, fixes her gaze on me. I hesitate, move closer. Closer again. She goes on watching me. I can see her eyes better now in the darkness. They look so weary.

'Mary?'

'Yes, my love?'

'Are you really dying?'

'I told you I was on the phone.'

'Yeah, but . . . I mean . . . like . . . '

'Like now?' she says. 'This very second?'

'Not this very second.'

'Today then?'

She's making fun of me now. Haven't seen this side of her before. Kind of playful. But we haven't got time for that.

'Mary, listen. Listen good. You—'

'I'm not dying today.'

'Mary—'

'Not planning on it anyway.'

She reaches out again, stretching for my hand. I'm close enough now. She can take it if she wants to. But she doesn't. She just holds hers still. And I know what she's doing. She's meeting me halfway. But only halfway.

I got to do the rest.

Yeah, OK. I get it.

Ease my hand out, just a bit. She keeps hers still, like she's making me reach every centimetre. Christ's sake, Mary, take my bloody hand, can you? But she doesn't. She just waits, watching my face. I reach out further, further—take her hand.

Her fingers close round mine.

Strangely tight. For some reason they make me think of Jaz's hand. Those little fingers. I've held them too. And they scared me just as much as Mary's do.

'You're in danger, Mary. Big danger.'

'Yes, yes.'

She doesn't sound bothered. Just tired.

'You got to get away,' I say. 'Away from the city. Far away. There's people hunting me and now they're hunting you. The police want to interview you. I heard it on the news. They think you might know where I am. So these other guys'll be after you too. And they're dangerous. They're—'

'Blade.' She's looking at me hard. 'Listen. It doesn't matter about me. What matters is you.'

'You matter too.'

She shakes her head.

'It's time for you to stop running. I told you that on the phone.'

'But—'

'You've done some bad things. You said so yourself. So give yourself up to the police. Take responsibility for what you've done. Pay the penalty, serve your time, start again. You're still young enough to have a future. Running's not the answer.'

'But those men—'

'Never mind those men.'

'They'll kill you,' I say. 'Maybe do something worse.'

'Do you think I care?' She watches me for a moment. 'Why do you think I stood up to them that time in the bungalow? And again by the warehouse. Do you think I'm naturally brave?'

'Yeah, I do.'

'Well, I'm not.'

She is, Bigeyes. Don't listen to her. She's brave. Trust me. She's one of the bravest people I've ever met. She was scared of me at first. And she was scared of the grinks. But she faced up to all of us and didn't flinch.

'You saved my life,' I say. 'And I want to save yours.'

'But you can't, sweetheart.' She squeezes my hand tighter. 'Don't you see? I've got a week or two left. Maybe just days. I knew I was on borrowed time when I first met you. That's why it was so easy to defy those men. What can they do to me when I'm dying already?'

'Lots of things.'

'Like what?'

I let go of her hand, stand up. I'm shaking but I

can't help myself. I reach over to the wall, flick on the light. Mary looks up at me, blinking. I stare back at her for a moment, then tear off my coat, sweater, shirt. Turn my naked back to her. She gives a gasp.

'My God! Who did that to you? Those men?'

'Men like 'em. And there's lots of 'em. More than you ever want to meet.'

She's silent. But I can feel her eyes on my back, tracing a path over the wounds Dig wanted to see. And I'm tracing 'em too, in my head. I know what they look like, every scratch. I've seen 'em enough times in snugs where there's lots of mirrors. I could draw 'em for you, Bigeyes, every detail. And I can do more.

I can remember how it felt when they cut me.

Mary speaks, quietly.

'Put your clothes back on.'

I do as she says, turn off the light, stand there.

'Sit on the bed,' she says. 'Hold my hand again.'

I do that too. We don't speak. We just sit in the darkness. After a while I realize she's crying. I make myself squeeze her hand, like she did mine. She goes on crying for a few minutes, then pulls out a handkerchief from under the pillow and wipes her nose.

'I'm so sorry,' she murmurs. 'About what's happened to you.'

'You're not doing so great yourself.'

She strokes the top of my hand with her thumb. Feels kind of nice. She wipes her nose again.

'If I tell you about me, will you tell me about you?'

I don't answer.

'I'll tell you anyway,' she says. 'You can do what you like. I don't need to know anything. I'm only asking because . . . well, because I care.'

I still don't answer.

Stop scowling, Bigeyes. You know why I'm not answering? Cos I can't speak, that's why. And why can't I speak? Cos I care too. You got that? I care too. So wipe that look off your face.

Mary goes on.

'I'm running from my family. Or rather, my sister.' She fixes me with her eyes. 'You make your friends in life, you know? But you inherit your family. If they're good, that's fine. But if they're bad, you're in trouble.'

'And you're in trouble.'

'Well, I was. Till I found Jacob again.'

Sound of a car outside in South Street. I flick back the curtain, check out.

'You're jumpy,' she says.

'You know why.'

'They're not interested in me, those men. And I told you, I'm not bothered about them. I'm more bothered about you.'

I check out the street. Car's gone past already. Didn't stop. I close the curtain again.

'Go on,' I say.

'Jacob's my twin brother,' she says. 'And my best friend in all the world.'

'Where is he now?'

'Sleeping in the next room.'

I glance towards the door.

'He won't wake up,' she says. 'Nothing ever wakes Jacob. He was just the same as a boy. I could fire this gun and he wouldn't hear it.'

I look back at her.

'What about the other rooms?'

'Empty.'

'All of 'em?'

'Yes. There's nobody else in the pub apart from you, me, and Jacob.'

'Does he own The Crown?'

She shakes her head.

'Friends of his do, people he used to know in Dublin. They sleep in a house down the road. Jacob helps out in the bar and restaurant and they give him free board and lodging. And me too now. For a few more days anyway.'

'Do they know the police are looking for you?'

'Yes.'

'Does Jacob?'

'Of course.' She squeezes my hand again. 'I already knew before you got here. I listen to the radio too, you know.' She leans back against the pillows, breathing hard. 'That's why I knew you'd come.'

'You didn't know for certain.'

'Yes, I did.'

'But how?'

She turns her head towards the curtains.

'Because underneath all that bravado, you've got a big heart.'

I don't speak. Don't know what to say.

'You don't think so,' she says, 'but you have. You're worried about what you've done. You're worried about me. You've probably got other people you're worried about too.'

I think about Jaz. Yeah, Bigeyes. I think about Jaz.

Mary looks back at me.

'My story's easily told. I own a farm in the south of Ireland. Just a small one but good land, great land. I inherited it from my parents and worked it all my life.'

'You got a husband?'

'No. Never married, never wanted to. I hired the people I needed and Jacob's helped me a lot too. We're close, you know? Like I say, he's my best friend in all the world. He's lived with me on the farm for most of his life and the business has done well, no question. But I've got no children to leave it to.'

'Can't you sell it?'

'I could.' She pauses. 'But I want to leave it to Jacob.'

'Does he want it?'

'Yes. Very much. He loves the farm. So I've put it in the will. He'll get the farm when I die.'

'So what's the problem?'

'My sister Louisa. And her husband. And the people they hire to do their filthy work.'

Another car engine outside. I don't look out this time, just listen. It's ticking over just below the window. Mary's watching me cute, saying nothing. Engine goes on ticking over, then suddenly revs up, powers off.

'Go on,' I say.

She gives me a quizzical look.

'Sure you want me to?'

'Course. I want to hear.'

'Louisa's the youngest of the three of us. And she's bad, really bad. Feckless, greedy, unstable, almost . . . I hate to say it . . . '

'Evil,' I murmur.

'Yes, I suppose so. Jacob won't have anything to do with her, and she's always been a little scared of him. That's good in a way because with him living on the farm, it's kept her away from me too. But since Jacob left to come here, I've had no end of trouble with her.'

'Why?'

'Because she wants the farm badly. She's always wanted it. Her husband's obsessed with it too. They don't need it. They're rolling in money. They already own lots of property in the area. But it's prime land and they want to exploit it.'

'So what happened?'

'They started by trying to charm me into changing the will, so that Louisa would inherit the farm instead of Jacob. They argued that Jacob was too old, too much of a loner, useless at business and so on, whereas they were experienced with property management. All that stuff.'

'Did you agree?'

'Of course not.'

'So what happened then?'

'They kidnapped me.'

'You serious?'

Mary nods.

'My illness did it. Made them desperate, I mean. It happened very suddenly. I'd been feeling poorly for a while but I hadn't said anything to anybody, then all at once I felt this terrible pain, went for some tests, and they told me it was cancer—inoperable. Got home, feeling stunned, desperate to tell Jacob. But I didn't know where he was. He'd come to this city to look up some old friends and maybe stay a few weeks. That was all I knew.'

She hesitates.

'Jacob's . . . his own man. Totally independent and he just kind of assumes everyone else is like him. So he's not the kind of person to ring every five minutes. And he doesn't like mobile phones so he hasn't got one. He said he'd get in touch with me when he had a definite address here, and I know he would have done in time, but when this business blew up, I hadn't heard anything from him. I didn't know who his friends were either so I couldn't get in touch with him to tell him I was ill. All I knew was that he was somewhere in this city. And I didn't want Louisa to hear about the cancer because I knew she might do something reckless. But she found out somehow. And acted at once.'

Mary's face seems to darken. She looks down as if to hide it.

'They came in the middle of the night. Not Louisa or her husband. They'd never get involved personally. It was some men, faces covered. But I knew straightaway who'd sent them.' She tightens her grip round my hand. 'They bundled me into a van and took me to a deserted house. Kept me locked in a dark room, no windows, no food, no water, no toilet. Then they worked on me.'

I can't bear this, Bigeyes. I don't want to hear any more. But she goes on.

'I won't go into details.' She's speaking low, forcing the words out. 'But as you can imagine, the object of the exercise was to make me change my will.'

'And did you?'

'No.' She looks up and there's defiance in her face. 'I didn't budge.'

Jesus, Bigeyes. Are you listening to this? I told you she was brave. And now I'll tell you something else. She's more than brave. She's heroic. She's got more spit than all the grinks in the world put together.

She narrows her eyes.

'And then I escaped.'

It's no good, Bigeyes. I can't deal with this. She stands up to those gobbos. She gets away. She rescues herself. Then she rescues me. I'm telling you, I love this old girl. I love her to bits. I haven't got half the guts she's got.

Her eyes are bright now, steely bright.

'There was a loose floorboard,' she says. 'I managed to prise it up with the heel of my shoe. Then I rammed the end of the board at the door handle. I had to keep jabbing at it but the lock mechanism was quite flimsy and eventually I broke it and got out.'

'What about the gobbos?'

'The what?'

'The men.'

'They weren't there. They'd gone outside for a breather or a cigarette or something. It was still the middle of the night. They obviously didn't expect me to get out and just left me in there with the door locked. I presume they were intending to come back but I didn't see them at all when I finally made it downstairs.'

'What did you do then?'

'I ran. Well, as much as a sick old woman can run.'

'To the police?'

She shakes her head.

'I had no proof of who my attackers were. No

faces, no names. And nothing concrete against Louisa and her husband. The most I could have claimed would have been that some men I couldn't identify had tried to force me to change my will in favour of my sister. I knew that wouldn't constitute evidence. I also knew Louisa would try to get at me again.'

'So you came here. To the city.'

'Yes. Since I've only got a short time to live. All I wanted to do was find Jacob and keep away from Louisa's thugs. The will's safe. Jacob'll get the farm.'

'Won't she just try it on with him?'

'What, you mean the charm and the intimidation?'

'Yeah.'

'No, because it won't work. Jacob's not scared of her. He's not scared of anybody. And he's got nothing but contempt for Louisa, especially after what's happened to me. He'll leave the farm to anybody in the world but her. And she knows that.'

Mary pauses, goes on.

'But the thing is—while all this drama was going on, Jacob knew nothing about it, and I was desperate to tell him. And spend my last days with him. He's all I've got left.'

She looks at me strangely for a moment.

'Well, almost.'

I'm not sure what that means.

She strokes my hand again.

'I haven't acted . . . legally,' she says. 'I've misled the police, given a false name and address, used someone else's bungalow. But the thing is . . . I had so little time. And I don't want to spend my last precious hours talking to police officers. I want to spend them with Jacob.'

She gives me that strange look again.

'Though it seems,' she adds, 'that I'm destined to spend some of them with you.'

'I'm sorry,' I say.

'I'm not,' she answers.

Silence. I feel kind of awkward. She doesn't speak. So I do.

'How did you get back to the farm after you broke out the house?'

'I told you. I ran. Luckily it wasn't too far. The farm was empty when I got there but I knew I wouldn't have long before they came for me again. I splashed my face, changed my clothes, and got my father's old gun from the drawer.'

She picks it up, turns it over.

'He only ever used it to scare off the crows. Used to fire blanks up into the air.'

She puts it down again.

'I took the gun and some blanks, scraped together a few personal things, then left. Made one big cash withdrawal from the hole in the wall in town, then headed off to catch the ferry to England. I haven't made any withdrawals since. I don't want to be traced.'

She shivers for a moment.

'Because I'll tell you something—while I'm still alive, Louisa will go on looking. She doesn't know I'm staying with Jacob but even if she's guessed that, she'll keep searching. You remember those three heavies who burst in on us in the bungalow?'

'Yeah.'

'My first thought was that it was Louisa's men. It never occurred to me they were looking for you.'

If only I'd known, Bigeyes. Christ, I could have helped her. I should have helped her. Why didn't I? And now I'm too late. She looks at me, smiles, and I can see she's reading my mind again.

'You couldn't have helped me,' she says. 'You had

enough on your plate. But I'll tell you something. That time in the bungalow, when I offered you—'

'A hundred quid.'

'Yes.' She frowns. 'I can't tell you how glad I was when you turned it down. That was pretty much all I had left.'

But she still offered it, Bigeyes. You cracking this? She still bloody offered it. I'm guilting up big time. I force myself to speak.

'How did you find Jacob?'

'He'd told me his friends ran a pub or a bistro or something. He wasn't quite sure of the details. Typical Jacob. He just had their phone number, which of course he didn't think to give to me. So I ended up trawling round every pub, bar, and bistro I could get to. And there are hundreds in this city.'

She takes a long, tired breath.

'I was getting close to despair. I can't walk much now and I could feel my energy draining away. When I found you lying outside the warehouse, I was checking some of the pubs down by the river. And that's when the miracle happened. Maybe it was a little gift from Providence for helping you. I don't know.'

'What do you mean?'

'I went with you to the hospital and while they were operating on you, I met Jacob. There, of all places.'

'In the hospital?'

'Yes.'

Outside in the street I catch another engine. Smoother than the others. A sleek, purry motor. Mary takes no notice of it.

'He'd just been to A and E. Can you believe it? Cut his hand with a kitchen knife and wanted it properly bandaged. We caught sight of each other at the very same moment. It was just . . . too good to be true.'

Engine's getting louder. Why'm I scared, Bigeyes? Could be anybody. The other motors weren't a problem. Maybe this one won't be either. But I'm still scared. Mary speaks.

'I was hoping you'd tell me about yourself.'

She lowers her voice.

'But I can see there's no time now. Because you're leaving, aren't you?'

The engine draws closer. It's just a short way off now. Can't see the car. Don't need to. It pulls over outside the pub. Engine falls quiet. Sound of a car door, another. Mary speaks again, softly.

'I understand.'

'Do you?'

'Yes.'

She holds my eyes.

'You want to lead them away. So they don't hurt me.'

She's right, Bigeyes. I don't want 'em to hurt her. I don't want anyone to hurt her. She leans forward suddenly, pulls me close, holds me. I feel her body shake.

'Take care of yourself,' she murmurs. 'And forget about me.'

'I won't. Ever.'

'Forget about me. Now go.'

She pushes me back. I look at her. I'm shaking too but I can't stop it. I want something I didn't think I could ever want. I want her to hold me again. She looks at me, understands, pulls me close again. I hold her back, tight.

Footsteps in the street, low voices.

I recognize one straight up.

The grunt.

Mary kisses me on the cheek, pushes me away again. I stand up, look down at her. It's the last time I'll ever see her. I know it. And she knows it too.

'I love you, Mary,' I mutter. 'I love you so much.'

She gives me a smile: a soft, sweet smile like I never had before.

'I know you do, darling,' she says.

I hold her eyes a moment longer, then turn to the door.

And I'm gone.

Down the corridor, tracking the sounds. Yeah, Bigeyes, I'm blasted in my head but I can still think. And I'm thinking just one thing right now.

Get those grinks away from Mary.

Doesn't matter about me. But I got to look after Mary. Like I got to look after Jaz. They're all I care about now. They're all that's worth caring about.

Footsteps in the street, tripping slow. I can hear 'em good, even from inside the pub. They've split. Grunt's gone right, other grink's gone left. I'm sure of it. I can hear the fat man's step easy. Plunk plunk plunk. He probably thinks he's creeping.

Other gobbo's gone quiet. Can't make out where he is. Wait a second . . .

Got him. Shuffly little step and it's already gone quiet again—but I know where he is now. He's down by the chip shop. I'm thinking hard, Bigeyes. Somehow I got to climb out, get to Dig's van, drive off, make 'em see me, make 'em follow.

Cos I'm the one they want. And there's still a chance they don't even know Mary's in here. Some screamer's tipped 'em off but it might be just me they saw. Hope so. Long as Mary stays safe, that's cute. But I still got to lead 'em away.

And now I got another idea.

Forget the drainpipe and back garden.

We'll use the front door. More risky but it's the grunt who's nearest and I could run round him on one leg. Down the corridor, top of the stairs, stop. Silence now, inside, outside, everywhere. Just the sound of my breathing, and my thoughts, loud in my head.

I can still see Mary's door. Closed, like I left it. But I can picture her inside. She's lying there, tense, worrying. I know she is. She's worrying herself sick about me. I got to go, got to get myself out of her head. And keep her safe.

Down the stairs, up to the front door, listen again. No sounds outside but I got to move now, whatever happens. If they know I'm in here, they'll be phoning for help. If they're here on a hunch, I still got a chance.

Push up the letterbox, peer out. No sign of anyone, just the dark street and the car they parked there. Big, shiny bastard, cool shit. Nobody in it. OK, so there's two of 'em. And one's the fat man.

Sound of footsteps plodding close. It's the grunt coming back. Ease the letterbox down again, listen on. He blobs past, walks on to join his mate. But the other guy's moving too. I can hear him. He's left the chippo and he's walking back.

Footsteps stop. Sound of talking over to the left, the grunt again and this time I catch the other voice. I know this gobbo. I've heard him talk before. Lenny, that's his name. Mean dronk, one of Paddy's old crew.

I know what I got to do. I know exactly. But I got to play stealth. Got to make 'em see me, but not coming out the pub, not like there's any connection. They got to see me some other way. But I can't move till I know which way they're going.

If they head this way again, I'm blitzed. If they go the other way . . .

They're moving.

Listen, wait. Still talking but the voices are fading. So are the footsteps. They're heading left. They're heading the other way. It's got to be now. I won't get a better chance.

Open the front door, soft as I can. I'm begging it not to click. It doesn't, thank Christ. Peep round into the street. Both gobbos down by the chippo. They've stopped walking, but they got their backs to me.

Ease the door closed. Again it doesn't click. What a beauty. Keep my eyes on the grinks. They're still facing the other way, talking low. Grunt's pulled out a torch and he's shining it down the little alleyway next to the chippo.

Slip down South Street, away from the grinks. Keep close to the buildings, check over my shoulder. They haven't turned yet. Yeah, boys. Keep popping your heads into that alleyway. On, on, towards the end of South Street, and still they haven't turned.

Just a bit further. Creep on, hugging the shadows, and now we're there. End of South Street just ahead, Wistler Road cutting off to the right. It takes us round the back of these buildings and joins up with the little side street where I left the van.

Slip into the doorway of the bank, check round.

They've moved away from the chippo. They're out in the middle of South Street looking up at the pub. Christ, Bigeyes, I hope Mary hasn't put her light on or something. They got to think there's no one awake right now.

And they got to see me.

Like I'm coming from somewhere else.

It's now or never.

Step out of the doorway, walk into South Street like I'm crossing it from Wistler Road, going somewhere else. Wait for the shout.

Nothing.

Christ, boys, wake up. Then I hear it.

'There!'

The grunt's voice. And now a thunder of footsteps. I stop, check round, make like I'm surprised. I got to do this right. If I duck straight down Wistler Road, one of 'em'll come on and the other'll cut back and come at me from the side street. I'll never make it to Dig's van.

I got to hesitate a bit, make 'em both come on, then blast down Wistler Road. I need 'em on my butt, both of 'em, not coming from opposite directions. But I can't let 'em get too close either. Lenny looks quick and you already know I'm not fast.

I run across the road, like I'm heading for the gate into the park, stop, dither, change my mind, run on, dither again, run back towards Wistler Road. They're coming on fast, specially Lenny, but I still need 'em closer. They mustn't split and plug me from two sides.

I make myself trip, roll on the ground, pick myself up again, and now it's time. Shit, it's time. I might have left it too late. They're pumping hard, eyes gleaming with triumph.

Dive into Wistler Road.

I've left it too late. They're much too close. I can hear Lenny's breath jerking out of him, the grunt heaving just behind. Tear down Wistler Road, right into the little side street, down that, pelting, panting, checking round.

Grunt's pulled up, gasping, but Lenny's coming on,

and he's gaining. Two duffs in the shadows ahead, digging in one of the bins. Lenny blares at 'em.

'He's got my wallet! Hundred quid each if you stop him!'

They straighten up, look at each other, edge across my path. I run to the right, pick up an old crate, throw it at 'em. One of the duffs moves back, other stands his ground.

'Stop him!' shouts Lenny.

The duff comes forward. Moves slow, scabby on his feet. I grab one of the bins. Empty, thank God. Pick it up, fling it at him. Thumps into the ground close by him. Duff moves back and I'm past, but I've lost time and Lenny's closer.

Much closer.

I'm not going to make it to the van. No way.

Another duff in front of me, an old gobbo, lurching, bottle in each hand. He's staring up at the sky, murmuring to the night. Don't think he's even seen me. Lenny calls out again.

'Stop that kid! He's nicked my wallet! Hundred quid if you stop him!'

Gobbo goes on talking to the sky. I'm on him

before he knows it, snatch the bottles, pull him round so he's between me and Lenny. Lenny clatters into him and they both fall to the ground.

Race on towards the van. I can see it now, just a short way down, and there on the right's the back of The Crown. Light on in one of the upstairs windows. Two figures standing there. Mary and a gobbo. Got to be Jacob.

They've seen me.

Jacob's talking into a phone.

But I got no time for that. Lenny's coming on again, faster than ever. Sound of a car revving up in South Street. Grunt must have turned back for the motor. I got seconds, that's all, seconds before he drives round and heads me off.

Up to the van, fumble for the keys.

Got 'em. Jerk open the door, check round. Lenny's storming in. I hurl the bottles at him. He dodges one, catches the other, comes on. I jump in the van, lock the door, crunch the key in the ignition, turn it, pray.

Engine mutters, mutters, mutters.

Start, you dingo!

It fires. I rev up, hard. Clutch down, first gear.

Thump against the driver's door. Lenny's there, face against the window. He's clutching at the van, swearing, spitting, belting hate. I start to drive but he goes on clinging there, pounding the side. I speed up.

Crash! The side window shatters and glass comes flying through. He's punched the bottle into it and smashed his way in. His hand's dripping blood from the broken glass but he's grabbing at my throat.

I step on the accelerator and he falls off the van. I see him in the mirror, rolling on the ground. Up through the gears, fast as I can. Got to get out of this street before the grunt drives in. But I'm too late. There's headlights in front of me.

Bearing down.

OK, fat man. If that's what you want. Flick on the headlights, full beam. Jam on the horn, ram the accelerator into the floor. Steer straight at him. Yeah, claphead, I'm ready to blow blood. Are you?

He's not. He swerves to the side like a dimp. I scream past, scraping his shiny toy on the way. His eyes meet mine—just for a second—and then I'm gone. Out into South Street, right, then left. Away down Tannery Lane.

And here come the grinks, quick as wind, tyres squealing as they chase my tail. They didn't lose a second. I'll say that for 'em. Must have jetted down Wistler Road and out that way. Check the mirror. Grunt's driving, Lenny's wrapping something round his cut hand.

No other motors in sight yet. Why not? And why's Lenny not ringing for help? Never mind his cut. He should be ringing for help first. But I think I get it. I can see it in their faces. They want me bad, they want me so bad. And they want me for themselves. This is personal.

And that's fine with me. Cos there's something they've forgotten, Bigeyes. Something maybe you've forgotten. This is my turf. Yeah, Bigeyes, my turf, my home ground. Not theirs, not yours, but mine. And you know what? I've had enough of running from scum. These two want me for themselves? Well, let's see, let's find out.

Who's chasing who?

Who's going to win?

Petrol's the big problem. Needle's right down now.

Maybe won't have enough to get back to the prof's house. But I can still crack these grinks. Long as I got enough juice to get where I want to go. And the porkers stay back.

We'll take the side streets.

Left into Morris Lane, right at the end, down to the market, on to Copeland Drive. Grinks still hot behind. Grunt's driving well. Can't say he's not. He moves like a pudding but he knows how to handle a motor. I'm not going to outrun 'em in this van. But I don't want to. Not now.

Over the cobblestones, left into Cartmel Lane, left again, right into Beaston Road. Check the mirror. Still on my tail, close as before. I can see the grunt leaning over the wheel, hunched like a bear.

Yeah, big man. I can feel your breath, your foul, grunty breath. And that's cute. I need you right where you are, you and your mate. Close, real close. I see the grunt's eyes harden. They've caught sight of me watching in the mirror.

I give him a smirk, then wheel right.

Down into King Street, right at the end, right again and down into Bellevue Parade. Got to watch it now.

Big, big road and there's bound to be porkers here. But I got to take this one. If I had more juice, we could go round but I can't risk it.

Check round. Cars heading both ways, lots of 'em, even this time of the morning, but I think we're cute. They're all muffins. I can tell. No porkers, no grinks. I watch 'em pass by. It's like they're floating, like they're from another world.

A world I can't have.

A safe world.

Bang! Van gives a jolt. Check the mirror. Grunt's nudged me up the bum. Thought he might try that. Yeah, dungpot, you're trying to blam me off to the side, maybe nip a tyre, make me pull over. Won't work. Cos we're turning off here.

Left down the sliproad, up to the roundabout, down into the underpass, through it and up again. Lights of the city below: streets, houses, shops, factories. Bastard river snaking off to the right. And in my mirror, the grinks pushing close.

I squeeze the steering wheel.

'It's time, boys.'

Left down the exit road, right into Waldegrave

Avenue, down to the bottom, right into Musgrave Road, and there it is at the end. Got it, Bigeyes? Stockland Heights. The big, black building at the end. It's a block of flats. Only there's no lights on in any of 'em. Know why?

Cos no one lives there.

Not even duffs.

You'll soon see why.

Slow down, sharp. Got to make 'em brake quick. No sweat if they ram me again, long as they don't stuff the van. But he's quick, that grunt. He's braked straight up and he's watching cute.

Wondering what I'm doing.

Got to make him think, Bigeyes. Got to speed up, slow down, mess about. Get a bit of distance before I bail out. If he's too close, I won't make it into the flats. But it's working. He's hesitating, just a bit. Thinks I'm maybe going to wig it from here.

Slow down again. Got to make him stop, but not in front of me. Mustn't let him cut me off. He's hanging back, like he's wary. Good boy, stay where you are. Stop the van, check the mirror.

He pulls up, just behind. Lenny gets out, grunt

stays at the wheel. Lenny starts walking forward. I rev up, power off.

That's it. Only chance I'll get. I got my foot hard down and I'm ripping through the gears. Check behind. Lenny's back in the car and they're coming on fast. But I've creamed some time off 'em.

Just hope it's enough.

Screech up to Stockland Heights, brake hard. Van squeals round and comes to a halt. Grinks are racing in too but I'm out the van and in through the entrance by the time I hear the clunk of their doors.

Up the stairs, dark all around. Glass crunching underfoot, smell of piss and beer. Sound of feet pounding on the steps behind me. I run on, up, up, fast as I can, quiet and loud at the same time. Quiet so they think I'm trying to escape.

Loud so they hear me.

Yeah, Bigeyes, they got to hear me. They got to know where I am.

Cos I'm going to finish this now.

Up, up, floor after floor. There's eight of 'em and we

got to run up the lot. Grinks are still pounding after me but I got to play this cute like before. Got to make sure they find me together. If the grunt's hanging back cos he's bombed, it won't work.

It might not work anyway.

I'm banging everything on one throw.

Run on, listening hard. Lighter steps closer up, thumpy ones further down. Grunt's starting to struggle. I got to think, Bigeyes. Got to make the fat man catch up. But there's no time here.

Lenny's too close. If I stick here, he'll get me.

Up, up, breathing hard now. I'm bombed out too, and I got Mary's face choking my mind, and Jaz's face, and sweet Becky's face. The Becky who died. That's there too. They're watching me, all three of 'em.

As I run on up the stairs.

Fourth floor, fifth floor, sixth floor. Lenny's still close but the grunt's gone quiet. I'm in the grime now. Should have thought of this. But I still can't stop. Got to keep climbing.

Grunt's started moving again. I can hear him. I reckon he's two floors down. I got to keep out of Lenny's way for a bit, let the fat man catch up.

Seventh floor.

Check round. Thump of footsteps still behind. Stairs ahead up to the top floor, corridor down to the right. Check again. There's still no time. I got to go on up. And if Lenny gets there on his own, keep out the way somehow, till the grunt joins him.

Up the steps, quiet now, soft as I can. Into the top floor corridor. Creep down, slow, slow. Rooms on either side. No doors anywhere. Been kicked in ages ago. Just shells here: black, smelly, paint-sprayed shells. It's like you're walking through a death's head.

And maybe I am.

Gone quiet behind me. That's good. Means Lenny's not sure, so he's thinking. That'll give Grunty time to reach him. Creep on. I know the room I want. I know it well. The room at the end. Best room in the block once.

But you wouldn't want to live there now.

Sound of footsteps again—two sets. They're coming up the stairs, both gobbos together. And that's cute. I need 'em to find me now. Stop, check round. I'm halfway down the corridor. Couple more seconds and they'll be through that door.

And then they'll see me. Like I want 'em to. But I'm shaking, Bigeyes. I'm breathing blood and I'm shaking. Cos this is it. Them or me.

There they are, in the doorway. Lenny and the grunt. I can't see their faces in the darkness, just the shape of 'em. They move down the corridor like walking shadows.

I stand there, watch, think. I got to do this right. If I mess up, it's over. Look right, left, like I'm checking rooms. Look back at the grinks. They're coming on, slow, steady, sure of themselves. Check the rooms again.

Turn and start to run.

Towards the room at the end.

No sound of running from the grinks. They're taking it slow, real slow. No rush now. They know I can't get out. Stop, check some of the other doors, look round again. Grinks are closer, much closer. They've speeded up. You know why?

Cos they can't wait, Bigeyes.

That's why.

And neither can I. I run on, down to the room at the end, stop in the open doorway. From inside comes a shiver of light. It's coming from the moon. It's reaching down and trickling in through the empty space that used to be the door to the balcony.

I turn back to the grinks, snarl at 'em.

'Which one of you wants to die first?'

They stop, both faces clear now, then laugh.

'Got your knife on you?' mocks Lenny.

'Yeah.'

'Let's see it then.'

I push a hand into my coat pocket. The grinks watch. But they're only wary for a moment. Something tells me they know I haven't got one. The grunt smiles.

'You must have left it behind, kid.'

I pull my empty hand out. Lenny smiles, then pulls out a knife of his own. The grunt pulls out a gun.

'Time to come home, little boy,' says Lenny.

'Piss off!'

I turn and run into the flat. The grinks follow, taking their time. I edge over to the far wall, feel my way round it, watching 'em close. They track me with their eyes. The grunt waves me towards the door with his gun.

'You're going the wrong way, kid.'

'Piss off, fat man!'

I see him flinch. I go on feeling round the wall, closer, closer to the balcony door. Lenny shakes his head.

'No way out there.'

I take no notice, move slowly on.

'I'm getting tired of this,' says the grunt.

'Then have a lie-down, fat man!'

He flinches again, raises the gun. I make a face at him.

'But you can't, can you, fat boy? Can't kill me. Cos you're not allowed to. You been told to bring me in.'

'I can do what I like with you,' says the grunt.

'You'll have to get me first, fat arse.'

He lunges forward, but I dart to the left, out onto the balcony. The moonlight's bright upon it now. I can see the city lights again, spread out below. Edge round the side of the balcony, close to the rail, watching the door.

The grunt appears first, Lenny close behind.

Not close enough. I need 'em together, not one in front. Grunt stops, looks over at me. I'm on the far side of the balcony now, back to the rail, grinks still in the doorway. The moonlight's so bright on their faces they look like ghosts.

I check out Lenny. He's still just behind the fat man. I got to do something about that. I need 'em together. I give him a little wink.

'Got no idea, have you, Lenny? How to hold a knife.'

He stiffens. I spit on the balcony floor.

'You're just a paid slug. No brains, no class.'

He takes a step forward, next to the grunt. And that's it, Bigeyes. Now's the time. I lean forward, crow at 'em.

'You're dregs, both of you! You can't kill me cos you've been told you got to bring me in. But you can't even do that.' I give 'em the finger. 'Cos you're dumb shit!'

They don't speak. They just rush forward.

Together.

I grab the balcony rail and cling on. It happens so fast I don't have time to think. There's a crumbling sound, a groan of timbers. The frame of the balcony judders, holds firm—but the floor gives way and both men vanish from view, like the moonlight's swallowed 'em.

I hang there, listening. Not a sound from either, not even a shout. Just a slow, heavy silence.

And a moment later, two soft thuds far below.

Van runs out of juice half a mile from the old prof's house. Didn't think it'd make it this far. Pull over to the side of the road, slump back in the driver's seat.

I can't stop shaking. Body's tense like it's never been. It's not those grinks. I don't give two bells about them. I didn't even check their bodies. It's all this other stuff. The stuff in my head. I got to think, Bigeyes.

Got to make up my mind.

Cos I'm cracking my brain. I got thoughts buzzing, feelings buzzing. I can't believe no one stopped me on the way here. I was driving like a dimp and I passed enough porkers. There's more out now than ever. And they must know about the van. Mary's bound to have rung 'em. Or Jacob has.

But I got here. Don't ask me how.

Out the van, start walking. Might help, might straighten me out. Keep well back from the road. Yeah,

Bigeyes, I'm not a total dronk. That part of me's still working.

Walk, walk, walk.

Feels good, feels better. No cars yet either. I'll slip out the way if I hear one. Walk on, think, try and think. Cos the thing is, Bigeyes, this is the moment. The crossroads. I knew that all the way back. It's been blitzing my head since those grinks fell from the balcony.

No, longer than that. Maybe since Mary talked to me on the phone. Maybe even longer. I got a feeling this goes right back through Mary, through Jaz, and all the way to Becky.

The Becky who should have lived.

Cos that's the crack of it, Bigeyes. There's too many nebs should have lived and didn't. And so many of 'em died cos of me. How many more's going to die if I stay free? I don't like to think about it. And there's people I care about now.

I don't want them to suffer.

Car coming, other side. I can see the headlights. Step off the road, crouch in the shadows. Car fizzes past. Out again, walk on.

See what I mean, Bigeyes?

That's my life. Creeping in and out of shadows. Ducking, dodging. I don't know if I can do that any more. I thought I could get away and play dead all over again. Now I'm not so sure. Not if I end up shaking like this, choked out of my head.

Mary's right. Running's not the answer.

So I've made up my mind.

I'm telling Dig thanks but no. He doesn't have to help me get away. Cos I'm giving myself up. I'll tell him he's got half an hour to clear his gang out the prof's house and then I'm ringing the porkers from there.

And I'll wait for 'em to come and get me.

Yeah, I know. Doesn't solve very much. Cos my enemies are still out there. And they'll find a way of getting at me in prison. There's too much stuff they want from me. There's retribution to pay too. I guess I won't live that long.

But I don't know if staying free's any better. And there's one other thing. One big thing. I'll be able to look Becky's spirit in the eye and not be so ashamed. And Mary's too when she dies.

And little Jaz.

I might even be able to face her too.

And that's why I'm going back to the prof's house first. I could have gone straight to the porkers but I gave a promise. To myself anyway. I'm going to finish that story for Jaz.

And then say goodbye.

So there you go, Bigeyes. Crossroads over. Walking's done it for me, and talking to you. Never thought you'd turn out to be useful. But you're starting to surprise me. And now here's another crossroads. A real one with a pub. Recognize it?

The Queen Anne.

Check round. All still. I'm glad about that. Not a single car since that other one. Everything's quiet, except . . .

Sound of sirens far away in the city centre.

Yeah, long way off. Just hope they're chasing someone else.

Over the crossroads, past the turning, up the lane towards the prof's house. Still quiet. Walk slow, walk careful. Riff's motor's exactly where it was. On, closer, house still dark, no lights at all. Looks just like it did when I left it.

Sky's lighter though, just a bit. Moon's still out but it's hidden by a cloud, and dawn's coming, soft and clear. Walk on, slow like before, checking round. Feels cute, feels OK.

So why'm I still shaking?

Stop, listen. Not a sound. Just the sirens again, way off, like little waily voices, nothing to do with me. Check the house again. Still feels OK but I'm shaking worse than I was. And I don't know why.

Walk on, round the side of the house, stop at the back door, listen again. Still silence. Try the handle—unlocked. Like it was when I left. Open, step inside, close the door. Silence everywhere. And then I get it.

Everything's wrong. Don't ask me how I know. I just do. I don't need to see anything. I can feel it like a frost. I want to run. I don't want to face it. But I know I must. Even if it's a trap, I got to do it for Jaz.

Down the hall, into the lounge, kitchen, dining room. No one downstairs. Stop, take a breath, back to the hall, up the stairs. Still too quiet. Nobody on the landing. Nobody in the bedrooms. Nobody in the loo or the bathroom. I got fear pumping now. Cos I'm telling you, Bigeyes, there's bad shit here. And I'm terrified for Jaz.

Only one room left, far end of the landing. The old prof's study. I used to go in there and read. Used to sit at his big old desk and pull down his books about Descartes and Kant and Sartre and all those clever gobbos, and try and understand.

What's waiting in that room now?

Walk down, slow, eyes on the door. It's closed. Stop outside, wait, listen. Not a sound inside, nothing I can hear anyway. Look down.

There's blood trickling out the room.

Step back, kick the door open, burst in. Dig's slumped against the wall, plugged with his own knife. There's nobody else here. I run forward, kneel down. But there's nothing I can do for him. He's finished. Then I hear it.

A whimper, close by. Can't see anyone. Another whimper. Check round and there she is, curled under the desk.

'Bex!'

She doesn't move, just curls up even more.

'Bex.'

She stays where she is, moaning now. I reach in, stroke her arm. She turns her face towards me, but she's got her eyes glazed.

'Bex, what happened?'

She doesn't answer. Don't think she's even heard me. But I'm wrong. She fixes me suddenly, starts mumbling.

'Xennie was acting weird. Wouldn't talk to nobody. Just kept wandering about the house and checking her mobile. And then . . . then . . . '

'What?'

'It happened so quick. Riff calls up the stairs and says Xennie's legged it. He's seen her out the window, climbing over the fence and running off down the field. And he says there's guys down the end of the lane, hanging about where we left the motors, and more guys coming towards the house.'

Bex shivers.

'Me and Dig had no chance. The others was all downstairs again but me and Digs was up here. We'd just got dressed again. And Jaz—'

'What?' I grab Bex by the shoulder. 'Tell me about Jaz.'

'She'd come up to look for us. When Riff called out, I was at the top of the stairs with her, giving her a cuddle. Next moment them guys come rushing in. Big heavy guys like we can't handle.'

I take a slow breath.

'What happened?'

She doesn't answer.

'Bex! What happened?'

She shivers again.

'Dig shouts down to the others. Tells 'em to split. Don't know if they got away, but I think so. I heard 'em climbing out the downstairs windows and running for the fence, the way Xennie went. And the guys in the house didn't go after 'em. They caught sight of me and Jaz up on the landing and come pouring up.'

I know why, Bigeyes. Christ, I know why.

Bex wipes her eyes with the back of her hand.

'Dig stood his ground. Backed us in here and tried to stop 'em. But what could he do? Eh?' She glares at me. 'Nothing. They just went for him and . . . '

She bursts into tears, talking wild.

'And I didn't do shit! I'm like . . . I'm crawling under the desk with Jaz and . . . I'm holding my hands over her ears and hugging her close so she can't hear nothing, can't see nothing, and then . . . and then . . . '

'Easy, Bex.'

'They all crowd round the desk, and one of 'em bends down and looks me in the face. And before I can stop him, he reaches out and pulls Jaz from me, and hands her over to some other guy, and suddenly she's gone.'

'Jesus.'

'She's gone!' Bex clutches at me. 'And I'm scream-ing after her. I'm just . . . screaming . . . '

She lets go of me, presses her face into her hands, then suddenly takes 'em away and looks back. And there's hatred in her face. Hatred for me.

'The guy reaches out again.' Her voice is bubbling with rage. 'And he clamps his hand over my mouth so I can't scream no more, and he's holding me tight, so tight it hurts. And I'm shaking like I never done before. And then he leans in close and he talks to me soft, yeah? Like we're mates. Calls me sweetheart. Says I got nice hair. Says if he was a bit younger, he'd ask me on a date. And then he gives me this little wink, all smooth, and he says . . . '

'I know what he says, Bex. I can guess.'

'Well, I don't care!' She glowers at me. 'Cos you're going to hear it anyway, you bastard!' She leans closer, spits out the words. 'He says . . . tell Blade if he wants the little girl back, he knows where to come.'

And she bursts into tears again.

I stand up, walk to the window, stare out over the garden. Dawn's coming faster than I thought. The moon's clear again and there's a tinge of grey on the horizon. Bex goes on crying and I want to cry too. I want to cry so much. But all I can do is listen to her. And the scream of thoughts in my head.

And the sound of police sirens.

Drawing close.

tim bowler

BLADE

FIGHTING BACK

In the next instalment of Blade . . .

Plum place, yeah?
Think again. Cos it's all wrong. It's zipping
you over. Everything you see, everything you
feel. Come closer, Bigeyes, and listen good.
This is big new grime. It's not like the old city,
the one we just blasted out of.
This is the Beast.

I look over the road. And you know what,
Bigeyes? It's weird. Like that other place is still
there. Like it'll always be there. Like you could
smash away all the houses, clear the rubble out,
turn the whole effing street into one great globby
piece of nothing, and you know what?
That part of it still won't be an empty space.
Cos ghosts don't leave that easy.

She's sprinting down the alleyway so fast I can't keep up with her. I let her race ahead. Doesn't matter, long as I can see her. She's running blind, like she was walking blind a moment ago, not seeing, not thinking.

But I'm doing both.

Checking the dark corners, the places to watch.

She slaps me hard in the face. I wince, but don't move. Didn't see it coming, but I see the next one. Other hand, whipping in. I let her hit me, and again, and again. She's still crying, great sobby tears, and she's lashing out big time, hard, heavy slaps, like she wants to split my face.

I stand there, take it, then suddenly she stops, half-falls over me, chin on my shoulder, arms loose.

'You bastard,' she mutters. 'I hate you so much.'

I've come back for Jaz. She's all I want. I don't give two bells what happens to me long as she gets away safe. But I'll tell you something, Bigeyes. If she's dead, there's something else I'll have.

My revenge.

Tim Bowler is one of the UK's most compelling and original writers for teenagers. He was born in Leigh-on-Sea in Essex and after studying Swedish at university, he worked in forestry, the timber trade, teaching and translating before becoming a full-time writer. He lives with his wife in a small village in Devon and his work-room is an old stone outhouse known to friends as 'Tim's Bolthole'.

Tim has written nine novels and won twelve awards, including the prestigious Carnegie Medal for *River Boy*. His most recent novel is the gripping *Bloodchild* and his provocative new *BLADE* series is already being hailed as a groundbreaking work of fiction. He has been described by the *Sunday Telegraph* as 'the master of the psychological thriller' and by the *Independent* as 'one of the truly individual voices in British teenage fiction'.